THE PAVILION IN THE CLOUDS

ALEXANDER McCALL SMITH

The
PAVILION
in the
CLOUDS

Polygon

First published in hardback in Great Britain in 2021 by Polygon,
an imprint of Birlinn Ltd. This paperback edition published
in Great Britain in 2022 by Polygon.

Birlinn Ltd
West Newington House
10 Newington Road
Edinburgh
EH9 1QS

www.polygonbooks.co.uk

9 8 7 6 5 4 3 2 1

ISBN 978 1 84697 586 8
eBook ISBN 978 1 78885 462 7

British Library Cataloguing-in-Publication Data
A catalogue record for this book is available on
request from the British Library.

Typeset in Sabon by Polygon, Edinburgh
Printed and bound in Great Britain by Clays Ltd, Elcograf S.p.A.

This book is for Alex Robertson

Part I

In Ceylon

I

The Chinese Poets Are Polite

This began in 1938, in what was then Ceylon, in a bungalow halfway up a hill. On occasion, when conditions were right, this house would be shrouded with cool mist, like thin, attenuated rain, and in this way would be made invisible from the plains far below. Around it, green swathes of hillside were covered with lines of tea bushes that stretched out, to disappear into scrub and jungle. Only human effort, patient and untiring, kept the wilderness at bay here. That task was endless, involving the imposition of a sense of urgency that was alien to the wisdom of this place – a negation of old courtesies, of ancient pride. Most people here came from somewhere else: from India, across a brief stretch of ocean, or from a remote source of men and ships, and the capital that was needed to get anything done.

So this made it a place of strangers, uprooted from elsewhere, and all aware that home was a long way away. The idea of home was something you carried somewhere inside you together with an understanding that you would never be fully accepted, even if you happened to be born in this country. And you had ways of compensating for that – by making the place you found yourself in seem as much like home as possible. And you invoked memories of home, and took comfort from them. For the Scots who worked there in the tea trade, these hills could be anywhere in the Western Highlands of their native land, remembered with longing on lonely, maudlin evenings, toasted at the annual Burns Supper in the panelled dining room of the Club, a landscape of the heart that they did not expect – nor particularly want – others to understand.

The bungalow was typical of its sort, of a style that had been planted, uninvited, across vast swatches of a rambling, already doomed empire. It was essentially British, but there was also something slightly Dutch about it, as the Dutch had been there too and had left their architectural mark in a taste for gables. The dominant feature, though, was the veranda, which was deeper than most, and which ran round three sides of the building, a dark mouth into which windows and corridors opened into shadowy interiors. Planters' chairs, with their swivelling extensions, appeared in clusters at various points on this veranda, allowing sunrise and sunset to be viewed from different vantage points. Beside each chair was a small table consisting of a brass-tray top and carved wooden legs. The brass trays had beaten into them designs of trailing leaves and the occasional helmeted warrior from an ancient epic, or an animal. One had a large and benign Ganesh at its centre, trunk and arms raised in benediction; another had the coiled shape of a king cobra, its hood extended, an exaggerated forked tongue protruding from its mouth.

"That tongue," Bella's mother said to her. "That tongue isn't the dangerous bit, you know. It looks like it, but it's the fangs you have to watch out for. The tongue is out like that so the cobra can smell. It smells with its tongue, you see."

She was very young, but they had already read Kipling's 'Rikki-Tikki-Tavi' to her, and the tale of the cobra and the mongoose had made a deep and unfortunate impression. They were just a bit too high in altitude for cobras, although they were occasionally seen. Kraits were a greater threat, and the pickers were sometimes bitten by these smaller but far more venomous snakes. She had seen a woman carried in from the hillside, her hand red with blood where somebody had cut at the wound to release the venom. "Don't look," her mother had said.

But she had, and she had watched as they bundled the woman into the back of a truck and started the journey to hospital in town.

"Will she die?" she had asked. She knew that her mother lied about death, because she said that nobody ever died, and yet she knew this was not true, as she had seen the funeral processions when somebody died down in the lines where the Tamils lived. And she knew that there were orphans, too, because somebody had pointed one out to her, a small girl who was always seen to be wearing a red dress, the only garment she had, and who was looked after by the woman who took the laundry away.

Now, of course, they said, "Of course not. Of course she won't die. The doctors will make her better." And then the warning. "But always look where you put your feet. Remember that."

The bungalow was a tea-planter's house on an estate called Pitlochry in the hills south of Nuwara Eliya. The name Pitlochry evoked the Scottish connections of the owner, Henry Ferguson, who had renamed the estate after he had purchased it two years before Bella's birth. Henry was a young widower who had come to Colombo as a man not yet forty, and had remarried within months of his arrival. His wife, Virginia, twelve years his junior, was the daughter of a Scottish shipping agent in Colombo. She had been born in

Scotland and had accompanied her parents out to Colombo when she was three, only to be sent back for education at the age of eight. It was not until she was eighteen that she returned to Ceylon, not intending to stay, but she had been immediately besieged by young men looking for a wife. There had been a boyfriend from a wealthy Burgher family, but his wild behaviour soon disqualified him before even his origins had time to be considered. Thereafter there was a succession of boyfriends, suitable and unsuitable, tolerated with grim stoicism by her father until, on her twenty-fifth birthday, he and his wife sat her down and told her that unless she found an appropriate man within a year or so she would be unequivocally on the shelf and would have to return home to train as a teacher. Their shock tactics worked, and when she met Henry, the son of a prosperous Scottish farmer, who had been advised to invest a considerable inheritance in a tea estate, she quickly made up her mind to accept the proposal that she sensed would not be long in arriving.

Henry knew as little about the cultivation of tea as he did about Ceylon itself, but he had been bored in Scotland and wanted a challenge. He arrived in Colombo and negotiated the purchase of an estate. He then engaged a reliable manager, who offered to teach him everything he knew, having been warned that growing and processing tea was an art which only experience could teach. You also had to have the right nose: if you could not pick up the subtle essences of the tea leaves as they were being dried or rolled, then you would forever be at a disadvantage. Quick decisions had to be made as to just when the leaves were ready for the next stage of the process; about just how much fermentation should be allowed; about just what degree of moisture could be tolerated at any particular stage, and in all of these the sense of smell was crucial. But Henry had that, it appeared, and, with his ear for language, he soon picked up enough Tamil for everyday purposes. That, he found, was the easy part: the workers on the estate were all Tamils, having been brought to the country from India, and their lives were governed by considerations of caste, custom and religion that could have been designed to perplex and defeat the outsider. But Henry was adaptable, and, hedged from the consequences of early mistakes by a combination of humour and Scottish stoicism, he not only survived his first couple of years in business but found that he enjoyed the experience.

Virginia knew that she was not in love with Henry when she married him, but she was sure that she liked him, and that, she thought, should be enough for marriage. And that liking, she felt, could mature into love, through familiarity – as long as one had other things by which to sustain oneself. Her passion in life was reading, and life on a tea estate was ideally suited to the pursuit of that enthusiasm. Like many women of her type and her time, obliged to live in remote locations because of their husbands' occupation, the challenge for Virginia was avoiding lapsing into inertia from sheer boredom. If that were to happen, then all that would be available to her would be gossip and complaint. Reading saved her from that fate, as did her decision to establish what she referred to as a *reading circle* made up of women from neighbouring estates and the wives of the odd colonial official stationed in the vicinity. This group met every three weeks to discuss books sent up to them from the bookseller in Kandy. Their meetings took place in a small pavilion that a previous owner of Pitlochry had built on the edge of the main bungalow garden, just at the point where the land dropped in a steep plunge of several hundred feet to the slopes below. The pavilion projected over the edge of this drop, supported by wooden pillars driven at an angle into the side of the cliff. This gave it the feeling of being suspended in the air, often above wisps of cloud that floated across the valley down below. Virginia called it the Pavilion in the Clouds, and had the name chiselled into the slab of rock that marked its entrance.

The reading circle was catholic in its tastes. They read Austen, Trollope and Dickens, but also such foreign and modern novels as arrived in Colombo on the mail boat. Tolstoy was popular, as was Stendhal. *Madame Bovary* had divided opinion, as had *Of Human Bondage* and *Sons and Lovers*. "I'm not quite sure where Mr Lawrence is taking us," Virginia had said to her husband. "It's all very unsettling. Do men really think that way?"

Henry smiled. He would read Lawrence one day, he said, but there was no time for him just yet. It was safer, then, to discount what he had to say. "I don't think so," he said. "I'm sure Lawrence exaggerates."

Virginia was determined that Bella would be brought up to appreciate books. She read to her every night, mixing adult reading indiscriminately with children's books. She had a taste for translations of Chinese poetry and would read from *A Hundred and Seventy Chinese Poems* even if the subject matter was far above her daughter's head. That did not worry Bella, who liked everything her mother read to her, and who thought of the Chinese poets as being exotic foreign uncles. She had a small family of stuffed dolls, and she named these after them. There was a Li Po and a Po Chü-i, and several others beside. She made a little black hat for one of them and said it was the hat given by Li Chien. Her mother said, "One day the Chinese poets will come and have tea with us. They'll come to the Pavilion in the Clouds. Would you like that?"

"I'll bake a cake for Li Po," said Bella, with all the solemnity of her seven years.

"He'd like that. And he might write a poem about it."

"Would he really? Do you really think so?"

"Of course he would. The Chinese poets are very polite. They always write poems for people who do kind things for them."

When Bella was eight, her parents engaged a governess, a Miss White, who had been staying with distant relatives on one of the largest estates up-country. She wanted to remain in Ceylon for several years, and few families would entertain the thought of employing a governess, but Bella's parents saw that engaging Miss White would save them having to send their daughter to the small boarding school at Nuwara Eliya. Miss White was a woman in her late thirties whose father taught at St Andrews University; he was an acknowledged authority, she said, on Victorian literature. She had worked in Calcutta, in the family of one of the Governor's most senior officials, and had then decided to visit Ceylon. She was punctilious in her time-keeping, insisting on four hours of study in the morning and two in the afternoon. For fifteen minutes each day she spoke to Bella in French.

Miss White was armed. Shortly after her arrival at the estate, she had gone for an evening walk along one of the paths that led from the sorting sheds into a forest area further up the hill. It was a path used by the Tamil workers and their families, and she had felt quite safe at an hour of the day when there were still women using the path as a shortcut to their homes on the staff lines. On this occasion, though, there was a wedding further down the hill, and the path was deserted.

One of the men on the maintenance crew had been fired

for insubordination to the overseers. He had been ordered to clear the room he occupied, but had declined to do so. The labour manager had been called and had promised to attend to the eviction, but failed to do so because it was his cousin who was getting married. The man had spent the afternoon drinking and imagining revenge for what he saw as the unjust treatment meted out to him. A poor head for alcohol had only deepened his smouldering rage, and when he came across Miss White on a remote section of the path he lunged at her blindly, pushing her to the ground and tearing off her blouse.

Miss White had fought back, gouging her assailant with her nails. In the course of the ensuing struggle, she managed to get hold of a small rock and struck him hard on the side of the head. This gave her the opportunity to stagger to her feet and flee headlong down the path to safety.

This experience led to her obtaining a small revolver, which she now carried in a shoulder bag whenever she left the house.

"Our governess is armed," Virginia told the members of her reading circle. "I believe she is the only armed governess in the country."

"She should have no discipline problems then," said one of the other members.

The ladies laughed. They felt sorry for governesses, who were drawn from the ranks of the unmarried and the unmarriageable. They were destined to be forever on the edges of families, their demesne the domestic schoolroom, their future one of contingency. And yet at the back of their minds was the thought that governesses might, for their part, feel sorry for *them*, thinking them untutored – which they often were – and dependent for their position on husbands, who could not always be trusted not to wander. At least a governess need not worry about how she looked and could become old and plain with an impunity denied to wives, even if she did not start off that way.

Miss White was plain, by any standards. She was thin, particularly around the face and neck, which gave her a rather odd look – like that of a puppet whose head is only loosely connected to its body, and operated by a different set of strings. She wore too much make-up – particularly rouge, which she plastered on her cheeks in two large pink circles. Apart from this artificial dash of colour, she looked generally washed out, as if she had been rinsed and hung on the line to dry in the sun for too long.

"Poor Miss White," whispered one of the members. "How sad that the only male attention she has received should be so clearly uninvited and unsuitable."

This was greeted with suppressed smiles. "I do hope," said one of the ladies, "she doesn't over-react with that revolver of hers if some rather more appropriate man should make a pass at her. There's a big difference between being slapped in the face and being shot."

Under Miss White's tutorship, Bella's reading progressed by leaps and bounds. She developed, too, a neat copperplate in which she wrote entries in her private diary that she hid under an old nightdress in a drawer. She wrote out, too, the names of the pressed flowers she mounted in an old commercial ledger, including the Latin and, in some cases, the Sinhalese names for each plant.

"Very advanced," said her father, with approval.

"I don't think one should pretend things are easy," said Miss White. "Education is a rigorous process. It is not possible to become educated without effort."

"No," mused Henry. "No doubt you're right." He did not recall ever having made much effort in his education –

such as it was. In fact, he was not entirely sure that he could describe himself as educated at all – not that it made any difference. You did not need to know much about history or geography or anything else very much to run a tea estate. Provided you knew about tea and its harvesting, he thought, had enough Tamil to be able to give orders and could prepare a balance sheet, you should do perfectly well, as he had done.

There were few children for Bella to play with – or at least few thought acceptable. There was the family of the Sinhalese accountant who was in charge of the finance office; they were Christians, and his two girls spoke excellent English, but their mother's own command of the language was weak, and reticence on her part prevented her from allowing the children to mix. There were other Scottish families on nearby estates – most of the estates were owned or run by Scots – and one of these families was not far away, on an estate called Inverness. They had two sons and a daughter, and the daughter was roughly Bella's age. But the two girls did not get on particularly well. Bella liked one of the boys, Richard, who, at ten, was two years older than she was, and whose company she enjoyed. There was something about him that intrigued her. She could not work out what it was, but when she was with him she found that she did not want others to be there. He made her feel strange inside – inexplicably so – and she liked to close her eyes in bed at night and think about him.

"I can see you like my brother," said the other girl. "You're in love with him, aren't you?"

She blushed. "Of course not. Who likes boys? I don't."

But she knew that this was not true. She did like boys. She did not know why, because they could be a nuisance, and they were often dirty; but she liked them.

To make up for the lack of human playmates, Bella

created personalities for her dolls. The two who were named after the Chinese poets, Li Po and Po Chü-i, were her constant companions, always with her, always watching what she was doing. They were both boys, she decided, and she had cut the long hair with which they had come and exchanged their dresses for masculine clothing. Li Po was the braver of the two and often had to try things before Po Chü-i would join in. Po Chü-i, though, was good at mathematics and drawing and had an invisible dog. They never fought, although Li Po sometimes accused Po Chü-i of being greedy and secretly helping himself to extra slices of cake. Li Po also had a pet whom only the two of them could see: a mongoose called, coincidentally, Rikki Tikki Tavi.

Virginia asked her whether she was enjoying her lessons with Miss White. "She's taught you so much," she said. "Your handwriting is so good now. And you've learned all those capital cities."

She did not reply, but stared steadfastly at the floor.

"So tell me, what is the capital city of . . . Now let me see, Canada? Yes, Canada. I'm sure you know that one."

"It's Ottawa."

"Of course it is. And what about Chile? That's a hard one. Could you point out Chile to me on a map?"

"It's in South America. Down at the bottom, on the left-hand side. And the capital is Santiago."

"My goodness! I'd probably have a bit of difficulty finding Chile myself. Not that I'm planning to go there, but still."

And then the question again. "And you like Miss White, don't you?"

There was something about the way the question was asked that put her on her guard. Did her mother want her to say that she disliked her? Was she being prompted to that answer? If she said she did not like Miss White, then the governess might hear of it and punish her. That sort of thing happened – she was sure of it. It was safer – far safer – to like everybody.

"Of course."

She noticed her mother's disappointment. But then, "Well, that's very good. It's best to like people who are teaching you things. It makes learning all that much easier."

Then her mother said, "Do you think Daddy likes Miss White too?"

She was not sure about that. Her father had never said anything about Miss White – at least not in her presence. She assumed that all adults liked one another, and she could see no reason why her father would be anything but well-disposed to the governess.

Virginia was waiting.

"Yes, I think he likes her."

The next question was put very gently. "Why do you think that?"

She shrugged. "He's never said that he doesn't."

"No, I don't suppose he has."

The subject was dropped. "Would you like me to read you Hiawatha?"

She nodded.

"From the beginning?"

A further nod.

She listened to the poem, lulled into a strange, dreamy state by the insistent rhythm of the tetrameter. She closed her eyes and saw the unfamiliar landscape she had seen portrayed in the illustrated edition from which her mother now read: the *shores of Gitche Gumee*, the *shining Big-Sea-Water*. But she opened her eyes at the warning and moved closer to her mother: "*Oh, beware of Mudjekeewis, Of the West-Wind, Mudjekeewis; Listen not to what he tells you; Lie not down upon the meadow, Stoop not down among the lilies, Lest the West-Wind come and harm you!"*

Why would anybody want to harm anybody else? What could the wind do to you?

She had had enough. "Now the bit about Minnehaha."

"Yes, that's a lovely part." A pause. "You'd like to be called Minnehaha, wouldn't you?"

"It's a beautiful name."

In Calcutta, Miss White told Virginia, with a certain air of reproach, she had lived with the family. "Of course, it was a very large house – not quite as big as Government House itself, but not far off it. I had a suite of rooms, and a small library of my own. We had meals in a small dining room – the main dining room was used only for special occasions. Of course, Colonel Summers could use Government House for entertaining when the Lieutenant Governor himself was away on leave and he was Acting Governor." She paused. "That was a busy time for all of us, when that happened. To be Acting Governor of Bengal is no small thing, as you can imagine."

Virginia listened, pained at the implicit comparison between the status Miss White had enjoyed in Calcutta and the one that she had here, as a governess on a tea estate, and not even the biggest tea estate in that part of Ceylon.

"We do our best," she said. "We make do up here. In my family home in Colombo, things were different. My parents sometimes entertained the entire Chamber of Commerce to dinner. And some government people too. Thirty or forty people."

"I'm sure that was very much appreciated," said Miss White.

"One cuts one's cloth as best one can."

Miss White looked away. "One cuts one's coat according to one's cloth." It was not clear whether this was a correction or an observation.

Bella was unaware of these tensions. She was relieved that Miss White was kind to her; she had heard, from Richard's sister, that at the small school they attended, the Hill School, they were told to stand in a corner if their fingernails were dirty or their exercise books blotted. And once, when one of the boys was heard swearing, one of the teachers had taken him and washed his mouth out with carbolic soap. Miss White only raised her voice occasionally, and then out of frustration rather than in anger.

The governess lived in her own house some distance from the main bungalow. It was a pretty building, although its veranda was tiny, and none of the rooms were quite large enough for comfort. It was also overshadowed by a stand of tall trees, inhabited by tribes of raiding monkeys. Anything left outside was in danger of being removed by these monkeys and carried up into the branches of the trees. A small boy was employed to keep the monkeys away, by shouting and throwing stones, but when he went off for a meal or was engaged on some other duty, they would take full advantage of the dropping of his guard.

Bella was not encouraged to disturb Miss White when she was at home in her house.

"Miss White does not want you hanging around all the time," explained Virginia. "She has you all the time for your lessons – she needs a bit of peace, as I'm sure you'll understand."

A formal invitation, though, was extended every other

Saturday, when Bella would go for tea with Miss White by herself. They would sit in Miss White's small drawing room and look at the photograph albums that the governess kept in a glass-fronted bookcase. These albums, of which there were fourteen, were mostly filled with pictures Miss White had taken in Calcutta, although one or two earlier ones were of St Andrews. The Calcutta photographs were largely of groups of people sitting in circles on lawns. Each photograph had underneath it a list of names, so that if memory failed, Miss White could look to the list and supply the details.

One or two faces appeared several times.

"That man," said Bella, pointing. "That one with the moustache. He's in lots of photos. Who was he?"

"He was in the ICS," said Miss White. "He was doing very well there. He spoke excellent Bengali, they said, although I never heard him doing so." She reached out to touch the photograph – briefly, fondly. "He was a very charming man with a wonderful sense of humour. He was always laughing. And he made other people around him laugh too."

"Did you like him?"

Miss White looked at her. "Did I like him?"

"Yes."

"Of course I did. Everybody did."

"What was he called?"

Miss White hesitated. "He was called Robert. We all knew him as Bobby. That suited him so well."

Bella watched her. Governesses did not cry, and yet she thought that Miss White was going to cry. Was she sad because Bobby had died, perhaps?

"Is he dead now?"

Miss White shook her head. "Of course not. Bobby's alive and well." And then she became business-like and snapped the album shut. "We should go and look at my vegetable garden. I had some of the biggest carrots you've ever seen. And there are some gooseberries that I've been growing. People said they wouldn't like it up here in the hills, but I'm proving them wrong."

When Virginia travelled down to Colombo, as she did every other month, Miss White had dinner in the main house each night. Bella would already have had her meal by the time the governess came in but was allowed twenty minutes or so with the adults before bedtime. Miss White always seemed to be in a particularly good mood on these occasions, laughing at Henry's stories and adding some of her own from her Calcutta days. These were peppered with references that Virginia did not understand, and that were usually prefaced with the words *You'll know what I mean, of course.*

In the darkness of her bedroom she could hear the sound of their conversation in the dining room, the low rumble of her father's voice broken from time to time by a high-pitched peal of laughter from Miss White. She felt angry: it seemed all wrong that her father should be enjoying himself like this when her mother had to go off to Colombo to see people who were no fun at all, as far as she could make out. They talked only about their illnesses and their pills, her mother had told her, and one of them insisted that she read out loud to them until midnight and beyond. They were very difficult.

One evening when her mother was away she woke up after only a couple of hours of sleep. From within the house there came the sound of conversation, fainter than usual, which suggested that her father and Miss White had moved into the drawing room, which was further away. She sat up and then, on impulse, slipped out of bed altogether, put on her dressing gown and tiptoed into the corridor outside her room.

She was now able to make out what her father was saying.

"He never saw her again . . . Not surprising."

Now came Miss White's voice. "You wouldn't have thought it, would you?"

"Hope springs eternal . . . as they say."

"He wouldn't do that again in a hurry."

Then there was silence, followed by a cough and the sound of a chair being pushed back along the uneven timbers of the floor. Something was said that Bella did not catch, and then her father's voice again, "I'll walk you over. It's a dark night."

She drew back into the shadows. The drawing-room door opened into the corridor, and they might see her if she remained where she was. She held her breath, and did not breathe in until they were outside. Then she returned to her room and crossed to the window from which she could look out onto the lawn. Miss White's house was on the far side of that lawn, tucked away in the trees, but lit by lights she must have left burning while she was over in the bungalow for dinner.

She saw two shapes cross the lawn, moving in and out of the shadows. She waited. A cloud crossed the moon, and the shadows intensified.

2

A Charming and Colourful Thief

Miss White said to her, "One day, of course, you will be sent home to school. It will all be very different then."

Bella listened, but said nothing. Being sent home was at the same time a threat and a promise. Home was somehow better – everybody knew that; it was a privilege; it implied membership of something that so many people simply did not have. There were the people who worked on the estate – she was not sure where they came from, but it was not home. They were *just there* – unknowable because they spoke a different language and had obscure beliefs. And that was all somehow ordained – a simple fact of life that everybody seemed to accept.

But she had never been entirely clear about where home was. She had really known only a couple of places – the nearby small town of Nuwara Eliya and then Kandy, more important, more bustling, not far away – and yet she knew that there was another country far away where everything of any importance came from and that was the *home* to which people referred. It seemed to be part of the natural order that the place you thought of as home – the house in which you spent your childhood – should not be your real home but something temporary, something you would eventually leave. You did not belong there – not, at least, in the way in which the Sinhalese belonged. They might have names that sounded Dutch or Portuguese, but that did not mean that they looked to those distant countries. Home for them was here in Ceylon, even if their names were van Horst or da Silva, or something like that: they were as Sinhalese as the Amerasinghes or Dissanayakes.

She did not see why she would have to go home. Miss White said it was for education – so that she could learn more about the world. And yet why could her governess not teach her these things that she had to learn? There was no limit, as far as she could tell, to Miss White's knowledge. She knew all the kings and queens of England, and Scotland, in order, starting with William the Conqueror. She knew all about the crusades and Robin Hood and Bonnie Prince Charlie and the building of the railways. She could recite Burns and Wordsworth without looking at a book. She had read more than ten plays by Shakespeare – she reeled off the list if you asked her – and she could quote long passages from *The Merchant of Venice* and *The Tempest*. How could there possibly be anything that any teacher in England or Scotland could teach that Miss White did not already know?

She asked her mother. "Why do people have to go to school in England?"

Her mother corrected her. "Or Scotland. Remember we're Scottish."

"I don't see what the difference is."

Her mother shook her head. "There are very big differences. There's nothing wrong with England, of course, but it's not Scotland."

"And Scotland isn't England."

"No, of course not." Virginia paused. "Miss White may forget these things, you see, because she's consorted with all those English people in Calcutta. That Deputy Acting Assistant Governor, or whatever he called himself – that sort of person. Sometimes English people forget all about Scotland."

"But why do I have to go to school there? In Scotland or England? Why can't I stay here?"

Her mother sighed. "Because this isn't our country. Do you understand that?"

Bella looked puzzled. The map that Miss White displayed on the wall of the schoolroom glowed with red: it was the colour of so many countries, and its meaning had been explained to her. "But it is. There's the picture of the King in the Post Office."

"The King, yes . . . It's our country in a way, maybe, but actually we haven't been here all that long. And there are not all that many of us. Over in India there are even people who want us out."

"Why would they want us out? What have we done to them?"

Virginia sighed again. "These are big matters. But the point is that children have to go home to school when they get a bit older. It's the same for everyone. That Macmillan boy – Richard – he's going in a few months' time. He's ten now, almost eleven, isn't he? That's very late. I don't understand why they haven't got round to it before, especially with everything being so tense with Hitler and Mussolini and these people. And the Japanese too. His mother was telling me they've booked their passages. She's taking him. He's going back to Scotland – to school."

Richard had spoken to her about that. He had said that he was counting the days until their departure. "I'll see you over there," he said. "When you come, that is." And then added, "Maybe. Who knows?"

He was going to school in a place called Perthshire. It was in the hills, he explained, and the boys all lived in large houses – far bigger than anything you could see in Kandy, where there were those missionary schools. The school had its own pipe band and even had a laboratory where you could study chemistry. "There are these things called Bunsen burners, you see," he told her. "You use them to heat chemicals. You have to be careful about explosions. There are explosions all the time."

She listened with fascination. She had seen a picture of a laboratory in her copy of the *Children's Encyclopaedia*, the mainstay of the small library of books in Miss White's schoolroom. There was an article in the first of the blue-bound volumes entitled "Why do I laugh or cry?" She had read that from start to finish and had even tried to explain it to Richard once, although he had not been listening. He had a habit of saying that he already knew things, and he did that now, although she suspected that he knew nothing about tear ducts, as she did. She had read the article one day – to herself – having taken the relevant volume out to the Pavilion in the Clouds. *There is no known reason why tears should come when we cry, but there is a very good reason for the tears we are really making all the time we are awake . . .* Richard should listen to that, because it might be useful for him to know such things. It would be all very well to learn how to use a Bunsen burner in a laboratory, and to cause any number of explosions, but you should also know about tear ducts.

Virginia encouraged her to read the *Children's Encyclopaedia*. "There's just about everything you need to know in there," she said.

But she knew that was not quite true. There was nothing

about the Chinese poets. She had looked for them, and they were not there.

"There's nothing about Li Po," she said. "Nor Po Chü-i. I've looked."

Virginia smiled. "Arthur Mee can't fit everything in. But I'm sure that if he asked Mr Waley he'd write something about them for him. There's no reason why boys and girls shouldn't read the Chinese poets. You do, don't you? Or, rather, I read them to you, and you like them."

Miss White said, "These Chinese poets lived a long time ago, you know. They are what I'd describe as *very* dead." She smiled – an icy smile that Miss White reserved for situations of which she did not entirely approve.

Bella was silent. This was plainly not true, and yet why should Miss White say they were dead if they weren't? Perhaps it was jealousy. Bella knew all about jealousy and how it could make people behave badly – even to the extent of them saying that Chinese poets were dead when they were not. She thought that if Li Po and Po Chü-i could hear about her dolls being named after them they would be pleased. It was an honour to name somebody after another person.

Her father was not interested in poetry, nor in the *Children's Encyclopaedia*. She thought that he knew a lot, but it was mostly about tea – a subject on which she believed he knew everything there was to know. He was a benign figure in her eyes, gentle in his manner, although she occasionally heard him shouting. That happened only when somebody did something stupid, such as allowing the water in the bungalow's heating system to boil. That was dangerous, he said. All that was required was that enough wood should be put on the fire to keep the water at a hundred and forty-nine degrees. That was quite hot enough for people's baths and for the shaving water he needed every morning. Why people had to stoke the fire until it was a raging inferno was beyond him. Did people not think about what they did before they did it?

She realised that Miss White admired her father. She noticed the way in which she looked at him from the schoolroom window when he was out in the garden, inspecting the orchids he grew under the trees. Miss White's eyes would follow him, as if waiting for him to do something. But he never would, because all that he ever did was to go to the tea office and the factory and then come home and drink a whisky on the veranda. It was the same with Richard's father – he had exactly the same routine. "He's very busy," said Richard. "There's a lot for him to do in the office. Write letters and so on. When I grow up, I'm going to do something quite different. I'm going to drive a Bugatti in races. Maybe be a soldier too. Who knows?"

"If you're a soldier you might get shot," said Bella. "You don't want to get shot."

"Not all soldiers get shot," Richard replied. "A lot of the time the other side misses. Then they get shot themselves. That's the way it works, you see. But I don't think I'll be a soldier anyway. I'll work in a laboratory, I think. Or be a surgeon, cutting people up."

She winced. She did not like the sight of blood.

"With an anaesthetic," he conceded. "I'd always give them an anaesthetic. That means they go to sleep and don't feel it while you're cutting."

The reading circle liked Rupert Brooke; Miss White did not. Virginia had mentioned that her friends would be discussing him when they came round for their regular meeting on Friday afternoon. Miss White had sniffed.

"He has his merits," she said. "But I must confess I find

him a bit precious." And then added quickly, "He's very popular – I'll grant you that."

But the damage had been done. Virginia affected to make light of the criticism, but her reply was barbed. "He's not for everyone, perhaps. Not everybody understands him, I suppose."

"Possibly," said Miss White, after a slight hesitation. "Although there might not be such a great deal in his work not to understand, so to speak. Of course, adulation of any sort is bad for writers, I think. It inures them to criticism." She emphasised *inures*, giving it its full value.

Virginia stared at her. *We*, she thought, *are employing this woman and yet . . . and yet she deliberately uses words that I shall have to go and look up.*

Miss White had not finished. "It's significant, I think, that Brooke's mother would have none of that sort of thing – wise woman. When somebody wrote an over-enthusiastic account of her son's life and said *he left Rugby in a blaze of glory* she changed *in a blaze of glory* to *in July*." She paused. "I thought that rather funny." And added, "Almost a zeugma, and it would have been had she said *he left Rugby in a blaze of glory and July.*"

Virginia remained tight-lipped, but her enjoyment of the Friday-afternoon meeting was dampened.

"You do like this poem?" asked one of the ladies, after she had read out, slowly and deliberately, 'The Great Lover'. "I find it very romantic. *The rough male kiss of blankets . . .* What an extraordinary line that is. So powerful."

One of the other members tittered. "I suppose that some of us understand that more than others."

They looked at her, and she blushed. "I mean . . ." she began, but the conversation had moved on.

Bella watched them from across the lawn. She was allowed to greet the visitors when they arrived but not to linger. And as for Miss White, she had never been invited to join the reading circle and made a point, whenever it met, of going into Nuwara Eliya to visit one of the nuns at a mission school there – a friend from Calcutta days.

It did not occur to Bella that Miss White was lonely. It seemed to her that the governess had plenty to occupy her time – she had friends to whom she was always writing, she had her gramophone and collection of records, she had her sketchbook in which she did her drawings of the birds that inhabited the high forests. Miss White was an accomplished watercolourist and had given Bella a framed picture of a blue magpie. *A charming and colourful thief*, she had pencilled in below the picture.

With all those things to do, you might expect Miss White to be too busy to be unhappy, but that was not the way it was. There was something about her, Bella thought, that made you feel sad yourself.

"Is Miss White unhappy?" Bella asked her mother.

"Why do you ask?"

"Because I've seen her crying."

Her mother was busy with her embroidery when this question was asked. Her needle paused.

"Really? Are you sure?"

"She was crying. I saw it with my own two eyes."

Virginia resumed her needlework. "People cry for all sorts of reasons. And sometimes for no reason at all."

"Like when you're peeling onions?"

"Well, there's a reason there. Onions contain a chemical that makes your eyes water. That's not real crying." Virginia hesitated. "Where was she? Do you remember?"

"Where was she when I saw her crying?"

"Yes."

Bella said, "She was on her veranda. She didn't see me. I was hiding in the rhododendrons."

Virginia shook a finger. "You shouldn't go into those rhododendrons. What about snakes?"

"They run away."

This brought a sharp response. "Snakes do *not* run away. I saw a krait there. You are *not* to go into the rhododendrons. People die. One of the pickers died six months ago. She died. That was a krait bite."

The warning delivered, Virginia returned to the subject of Miss White. "Why do you think she was crying? Did you speak to her?"

She shook her head. "I didn't. After a while she got up and went inside."

Virginia looked thoughtful. "It wasn't anything you did? You haven't been difficult, have you?"

There was a firm denial. "It's not my fault."

"Because her job is hard enough as it is," Virginia went on. "You wouldn't want to make it even harder."

"I think sometimes she's sad when Daddy doesn't talk to her."

At first Virginia was silent. The needle moved into the embroidery; the thread was tightened. Then, "Did she tell you that?"

"No, but I can tell. I can tell from the way she looks out of the window when Daddy is in the garden."

"I see."

Virginia put the embroidery aside. "I'm going to go for a walk."

"May I come too?"

"No. I want to go by myself. We'll go for a walk together tomorrow."

Virginia left the house. A path led through the garden and then disappeared up the slope directly behind the property to join, higher up, the path on which Miss White had met her assailant. There were points on this path that afforded views of the entire hillside below, green upon green, stretching out to lower summits. When the cloud came in, those summits would protrude above the mantle of cloud that cloaked the lower ground. They would be to all intents and purposes like little islands in a white sea stretching out to a distant horizon.

She went over what she could do. She was unwilling to talk directly to Henry, as she could not bring herself to make any accusations, particularly ones for which she had no evidence. Bella's view of what was happening was a child's view – and children got these things wrong. They observed the adult world from down below but did not really understand it. But if a wife failed to act, then she could hardly blame anybody if things got out of control. Men were weak: even the best of men – and Henry was a decent man, by any standards – could be tempted by a younger woman, especially one who was a member of the household. There was nothing new in that; in fact, it was a very old story. And if she felt that she could not talk directly to Henry about it, then she could talk to Miss White. She could confront her and tell her that it would be best, all things considered, if she sought alternative employment. That was a polite way of firing somebody, and they would, of course, give her excellent references, particularly if Miss White put in her resignation herself. Now that she thought of it, it occurred to her that she could do all this without Henry even hearing about any of the background. She would be as surprised as anybody. "Governesses tend to do this sort of thing," she might say. "They don't stay."

By the time she reached the first vantage point on the path, her mind was made up. Henry had directed the Tamil gardeners to create a small clearing in which a stone bench had been constructed. She sat on this now and looked down over the tea gardens climbing up the hillside. A line of women moved slowly along the bushes, baskets on their backs. They did that all day, every day throughout the year, with the exception of a few begrudged religious holidays. That was their lot. And her lot, it seemed, was to sit on this stone bench and watch them. That came about through an accident of birth; through good fortune; through the operation of karma. But just about everything came about in that way, if one thought about it: where you started was almost always where you ended up, except in a few unusual cases, where effort or sheer luck overcame disadvantage. That had happened to Thomas Lipton, whose house was not all that far away. He had been born in the Glasgow Gorbals, in the humblest of circumstances, and had risen to the top of the tea world through his own efforts. The boy who started off as a messenger, running errands, ended up consorting with presidents and princes. By contrast, she had done nothing to deserve what she had, and might be viewed askance by some for that precise reason. But at least the Tamils, with their Hinduism, would not resent her for her easy life, she thought. That was the great attraction of a belief in reincarnation, at least to those born to ease and privilege: it justified what you had and what others did not have.

She rose from the bench. The walk had cleared her mind, and she had decided what she was going to do – or rather, what she was not going to do. She would see how the situation developed. She would not do anything precipitate, but she would be vigilant. She would watch Miss White and act only if it became necessary. If the governess put one foot wrong, she would deal with her. There were plenty of others who could take the job and who would, she imagined, resist any temptation to condescend to her intellectually; who would not use the word *inure* with a view to confusing her; who would not send predatory looks in her husband's direction. There was no shortage of such people, and any one of them could easily be engaged to see Bella through to the next milestone in her education.

She *felt* better for her decision. In one sense she was threatened by Miss White; in another she thought that magnanimity was the least that was required of her. She had so much in this life – money, a husband, a child, a house in the clouds – and the self-assurance that came from the possession of all of these advantages, whereas Miss White had so little: a tenuous position, held at the pleasure of others; no man to support her; single status that kept her on the periphery of so much; and very modest talents, in spite of ill-concealed displays of patchy learning. Even her father, whom she referred to as *my father, a member of St Andrews University,* was not quite the scholar she made him out to be. Where were his books? She had asked Miss White whether he had written anything they might discuss in her reading circle – she knew that he had not – and her question had gone unanswered.

So poor Miss White might be tolerated and her faults overlooked. That was the right thing to do; it was a turning of the cheek from which a warm glow of satisfaction might be derived. And it could always be reviewed should Miss White get up to anything – which was still possible, although rather improbable.

She walked back to the house. She would call in at Miss White's bungalow and offer her tea. Kindness cost nothing, was simple to perform and was noticed, she imagined, by the Recording Angel – if such an unlikely being existed, which was highly doubtful. The Recording Angel was actually within us – as our conscience: that was the modern view, and one to which she could subscribe. She approached Miss White's door with resignation, as one who has a duty to perform but is not looking forward to it. She was beginning to resent the governess, and for a moment her charitable impulse wavered – to the point where she almost turned round and went on, instead, to her bungalow.

3

If You Were Riding in a Coach

Bella had put Li Po and Po Chü-i on the windowsill of her
bedroom. The two dolls were seated side by side, like the
old friends they were, looking out over the lawn towards the
Pavilion in the Clouds. It was early evening, and the last of
the sunlight was touching the top of the pavilion's pagoda
roof. Dusk came quickly, and in no more than ten minutes or
so the evening sky would have begun to darken.

"Are you hungry?" Bella asked Li Po. "Because I am."

Li Po was silent. His painted face was, as ever, impassive.
He was not one to reveal his feelings – unlike Po Chü-i, whose
temperament, Virginia had decreed, was a stormy one.

"You can have more rice if you like," said Bella, and
passed a tiny invisible plate on which imaginary rice had
been heaped.

"It has all the things you like to have in your rice," she
said. "Boiled fish. And peas. And a bit of ginger. You like
ginger, Li Po."

Li Po did not dispute that.

Bella looked out of the window, past the dolls.

"See?" she said. "See over there? That's Miss White,
walking across the lawn. You know her, I think. You've
heard her talking French. She thinks you don't understand

French, but I know you do. You understand everything because you're very clever."

Halfway across the lawn, Miss White stopped to look up at the sky. The pale round disc of the moon was floating up now from the horizon, as light as a balloon, its faintness and delicacy contrasting with the vivid colours it gazed upon below – the dark greens of the vegetation, the red-brown of the land where the earth had been scarred by earthworks, the sharp blue of the distant hills. She stood still for a moment, watching the moon inch up the sky, before she continued towards the Pavilion in the Clouds.

Bella observed Miss White going into the Pavilion. She expected her to sit down in one of the wicker chairs arranged in a crescent for people to admire the view, which was what adults liked to do, but she did not, going forward instead to stand at the parapet and look down over the canopy of tree-tops far below. Bella did not like to see people do that, at least not while she was standing nearby, as she had no head for heights and was frightened by the sheer drop below.

She turned to speak to the dolls. "Would you like me to read to you?" she asked.

Li Po inclined his tiny, stuffed head. Po Chü-i conveyed his response through his eyes, which were small painted dots. He had no objection.

She had her own copy of *A Hundred and Seventy Chinese Poems* now, a gift from her mother for her eighth birthday. She fetched this from the bookcase beside her bed before retrieving the dolls from the windowsill and seating them on the rug in the centre of the floor.

She chose a poem she liked. Many meant little to her, although she loved the sounds of the words. Some, though, she understood, and this ode to friendship was one such. She read it solemnly, pausing after each line before proceeding to the next:

> If you were riding in a coach
> And I were wearing a coat of straw,
> And one day we met in the road,
> You would get down and bow.
> If you were carrying a cheap umbrella
> And I were riding on a horse,
> And one day we met in the road
> I would get down for you.

Her mother had explained it to her. "This means that even if the poet were rich and his friend were poor, he would still be his friend. You understand that, don't you?"

To begin with she had not, but then the truth of the poem had dawned on her, and she nodded.

"So, a person who's strong should be nice to a person who's weak," her mother continued. "Yes, it means that too. It doesn't matter what's on the outside – what counts is what's on the inside."

The dolls listened. They were the most uncomplaining of audiences. And now she let them sit closer together, and she put Li Po's arms around Po Chü-i, so that they looked like two old friends comforting one another. They had no secrets from one another, she said, and they had promised to live with one another until the day they died. Nothing would ever part them.

She lay down on the rug and looked up at the ceiling. The room was in semi-darkness now, because she had not switched on a lamp, although the generator that provided electricity for the whole estate could be heard thudding away in its shed. It was turned on promptly at sunset by the man who then walked down the path to stoke the fire for the hot-water boiler, and it would remain on until nine o'clock, when everyone would have retired to bed. After that, tilly lamps would be used, especially for reading, for which their hissing white light was so suitable.

She shivered.

"It's cold now," she said to the dolls. "You'll need to put on more clothes."

She had several spare outfits for the dolls, including padded jackets of the sort that she knew Chinese poets liked to wear. Some of the *A Hundred and Seventy Chinese Poems* made reference to the cold, especially up in the mountains – like everybody else, the Chinese poets preferred the warmth of summer to the harshness of winter. Now she took the minute padded jackets out of a drawer and put them on the dolls, taking care with the stitching, which was apt to give way if put under stress. Then she added miniature felt boots that she herself had made, easing them over the dolls' feet, and a small striped scarf for Li Po and a chequered one for Po Chü-i.

She got up off the floor and crossed to the window. The night had descended while she was playing with the dolls, and the kitchen window of Miss White's house was now lit up. She saw a movement within – a dark shape – before a blind was drawn. She thought that Miss White must be in the kitchen, preparing her meal. She was a good cook and would spend hours making meals that she would then eat alone, seated on the veranda, looking out towards the hills. Bella did not like the dishes Miss White made, as they were too hot and spicy for her taste. "I acquired my palate for curries in Calcutta," Miss White said. "The hotter, the better. There was a marvellous chef at Government House, when we went there for dinner. The Governor loved hot curries.

They couldn't be hot enough, from his point of view."

And then she heard a scream. It was sudden, and piercing, and it was accompanied by a loud report – like the firing of a gun. And then there was silence.

She pushed open the door of her room and ran down the corridor towards the kitchen. Her father was still at the tea office – he often did not return until the last minute before dinner, which was still half an hour away. Her mother might be in the kitchen: she liked to be there to supervise the cooking of dinner by Michael, the Christian Sinhalese cook. Michael worshipped her mother, and she found his company reassuring and restful.

But she was not there. Michael had heard the scream and was struggling to get out of his apron.

"There is something happening," he said, turning to the young boy who was his assistant in the kitchen. He snapped out an order to fetch the boss from the tea office, and the boy ran out, barefooted.

They went out onto the lawn.

"Where is your mother?" asked Michael.

She did not know. She did not want to acknowledge the scream to have come from her, although she knew it was likely. Who else was there to scream like that? Miss White? But she had appeared on her veranda now and was calling out to find out what was wrong.

Michael had a torch, and he shone this round the lawn while he called out.

There was a cry from the darkness around the Pavilion, and Michael began to run in that direction. Miss White came too, the white sari in which she wrapped herself flapping eerily in the darkness.

The beam of the torch played on the Pavilion as Michael crossed the lawn. Bella stared fixedly into the darkness, trying to make sense of what she was seeing. The front barrier had collapsed and was leaning drunkenly over the edge, still attached to the rest of the Pavilion, but only by shattered wooden tendons.

Miss White ran after Michael. "She must have fallen over," she called out.

Bella was mute with horror. She stood quite still, too frightened to go into the Pavilion to see what had happened. Michael and Miss White, though, were peering over the edge of the structure, shining the torch down into the void.

Michael cried out. "Lady, Lady! We can see you."

There was an answering shout from below, and Bella gasped as she realised that her mother was still alive. She closed her eyes, though, and remained where she was. She could not bear the thought of looking down onto the undergrowth that had presumably broken her fall. Had it not been for the trees that clung to the steep drop of the hillside, she would have fallen several hundred feet to the rocky floor of the valley.

Henry arrived, accompanied by three men, all bearing torches, all shouting out to one another and to Michael. Two of the men were dispatched to fetch ladders and ropes while the third stayed with Henry.

Miss White was shaking. "She hasn't fallen too far," she said to Henry, her voice strained and high-pitched. "She seems to have been caught by the trees."

Henry nodded. "They're bringing ropes," he said. And then, "You take Bella inside."

Miss White nodded and came over to Bella's side. "Mummy will be fine," she said, struggling to keep her voice even. "You mustn't worry. They'll rescue her."

Bella half opened her eyes and then shut them again. She

did not want this to be happening. By closing her eyes, it seemed to her that she was shutting it out – making it seem less real, as one could do with inexplicable shadows in the bedroom at night. If you closed your eyes, the shadows were lost in the general darkness and became less threatening.

Virginia was in no fit state that night to explain what had happened. The estate employed a nurse to run a small clinic for the Tamil families, and she was summoned to tend to Virginia once they brought her up the side of the cliff, strapped to a stretcher. The nurse tended to a laceration on her right forearm and scratches around her neck. She was worried, though, about Virginia's leg, which she bound up in a splint while they waited for the doctor to arrive from Nuwara Eliya.

It was almost ten by the time the lights of Dr Pereira's car were seen on the winding road up to the estate. Henry met him and took him into the room where Virginia was lying on a day bed, the nurse at her side. The doctor gave the nurse a cursory nod and began his examination. He agreed that the leg should be X-rayed – just in case.

"It would be best to take her down to Kandy," he said. "They have the equipment, and there's a good surgeon there."

Henry was concerned by the mention of surgery.

"It depends on whether there's a fracture in the leg," said Dr Pereira. "If there is, they sometimes have to operate. We'll have to wait and see." The doctor frowned. "She fell, you say?"

Henry nodded. "We have a summer house on the edge of the cliff. The barrier gave way."

The doctor shook his head. "She's very fortunate. It's a long way down."

"The trees broke her fall about thirty or forty feet down," said Henry.

The doctor raised an eyebrow. "How did it happen?"

Henry glanced at Virginia. The doctor had administered morphine, and she seemed to be dozing off. He shrugged. "I don't want to bother her right now," he said.

Dr Pereira agreed. "Of course not. All in good time."

They carried Virginia out on a stretcher, helping her into position in the back of the car, where her sore leg could be propped up on pillows. Then the nurse joined Henry in the front, and they set off for Kandy. Miss White comforted Bella, putting her arm about her and leading her back to her bedroom. "She'll be as right as rain in a day or two," she said. "There's nothing to worry about."

"Will you stay?" asked Bella.

"Of course. I'll get my things, and I'll sleep in the spare room."

Bella was reassured by Miss White's presence. It took her some time to drift off to sleep, though, as she kept going over what she had seen: the shattered barrier, the beam of the torches probing the darkness, her mother's look of confusion as they manhandled her stretcher across the lawn.

She turned to Li Po and Po Chü-i, whom she had placed on the pillow beside her. They were comforting. Li Po had seen this sort of thing before, of course; you should always be careful with heights, he said. Po Chü-i agreed. Heights and water, he whispered – you had to treat both with grave respect.

"It was an accident," said Bella.

Li Po said nothing; he could just have been too tired to speak, or his silence could have signalled agreement – she could not tell which it was.

Virginia came home two days later. She had been badly scratched and had sprained a muscle in her leg – nothing was broken – but there had been some concussion, though, and the hospital had wanted to keep her under observation until satisfied that it was safe for her to return. She had been fortunate, they said a twig from the tree had penetrated the skin around her neck and had narrowly missed an artery: half an inch in the other direction would have brought about a very different outcome.

She took the news of the narrow escape philosophically. "No point in losing sleep over a near miss," she said. "All of us have those. We turn left rather than right and miss the car that would otherwise have run us over. We slow the car to look at a view and miss the lorry that would have collided with us on the next bend. At the last moment we change our booking on a ship that sinks with the loss of all on board. And so on."

"So not only cats have nine lives," said Henry.

"Exactly."

"Tell me exactly what happened," he said.

"It's a bit of a blur," she replied. "But I do remember being in the Pavilion, of course: I'd gone out because I wanted to see the Southern Cross."

He nodded. They called it *their constellation* and looked for it together at the right time of the year, when it would be hanging down low over the horizon, pointing south. To them it was a promise of something better: of Australia and New Zealand, where life would be so much easier. He had been offered a half share in a sheep station in New South Wales and had turned it down – a decision he bitterly regretted. The Sinhalese would want them out sooner or later, he thought, no matter what people said. The Portuguese had been here and had gone, and the same was true of the Dutch. The British should not fool themselves into thinking they would be any different. If they had gone to Australia, at least they would have belonged. But it was too late now.

"Did you lean against the balustrade?"

"The barrier? Yes, I must have. I don't remember doing that, though."

"You wouldn't. A major shock can wipe out memory of what happens. That's not unusual."

She sighed. "I must have. I must have leaned a bit too far forward to see the stars. And then . . . That's the bit I don't really remember. I suppose I remember a bit of a noise – a sort of crack, rather like a firework going off . . ."

"Or a gun?"

"Yes, a bit like that." She paused. "Though it can't have been a shot. It must have been the wood splitting."

"I imagine so."

"And then I don't really remember much after that. I felt the trees around me; there were leaves in my face and eyes. And there was a pain in the leg. Then I think I went to sleep. That sounds unlikely, though, doesn't it?"

"Concussion," he said. "It can be like dropping off to sleep."

He was silent for a while as he thought of what she had said. Then he continued, "It's a mercy that it was you."

She looked surprised. But then she smiled. "I see what you mean."

"I put it rather tactlessly," he said hurriedly. "What I mean is that it was a mercy that it was one of us rather than Bella."

"Of course. Of course."

"And had it been me," he went on, "The trees might not have borne my weight. You might be a widow today."

She shook her head. "Please don't talk like that."

"Sorry, I was just thinking." He held her hand. "My blood runs cold to think that Bella was playing right in front of that barrier just a few hours before it happened. It could have given way then."

"But didn't."

He was ready to blame himself. "I should have had it checked. I should have made sure it was secure enough."

She reassured him that he should not reproach himself. There was no reason to imagine that the barrier was about to give way – it had looked safe and sound in every respect.

"I'm very sorry about it," he said. "We were all using the Pavilion – you, me, Bella – and I had no idea it was unsafe. I was in it the day before, and you . . . when were you in it last? Did you see anything?"

She hesitated before replying – and she started with a repeat of his question. "When was I in the pavilion?"

He nodded. "Yes. I wondered if you noticed anything."

She shook her head. "I hadn't been in it for two or three days. Wednesday, I think, when I had tea in it with Bella. I was reading to her from Lamb's *Tales from Shakespeare.*" His eyes fell upon her, and she looked away. "No," she said. "I saw nothing then."

He was watching her, as if he were waiting for her to add something. But she did not. Then he said, quietly, "I see." And after a moment or two he added, "Sudden structural failure."

"What's that?"

"Materials just fail. They reach the end of their life. Like people do." He swallowed these words, realising that they might sound tactless at a sick bed. "Sometimes vibration causes it. And they break. Nobody may be expecting it, but it can be catastrophic." He paused. "The Tay Railway Bridge.

Remember that one? A train was on it at the time, and the whole structure just gave way."

"I'm something lighter than a train, I think."

He smiled. "I'd never compare you to a train."

"Just as well." The morphine that she was still taking made her feel pleasantly drowsy. "Shakespeare might have written something quite different, you know."

He looked puzzled.

"*Shall I compare thee to an express train?*"

"No," he said. "I don't think so."

She waited for him to laugh, but his mind was on other things.

4

Trapped in Ignorance

On the morning of her mother's return from hospital in Kandy, Bella woke up to find that Li Po and Po Chü-i had both fallen out of bed. It was not unusual for one of the dolls to slip off the edge of the bed and be discovered on the floor the next morning, but it was rare for this indignity to be visited upon both of them.

"You poor things," she said, scooping them up and dusting them off. "The ants might have carried you away in the night."

The dolls took this as a joke, which she expected they would. There were ants that occasionally invaded her bedroom from a ventilation grille at the edge of the floor, but they had business of their own and disappeared as quickly as they arrived. No, Li Po and Po Chü-i were in no danger of anything on the floor, other than a dent to their pride.

She dressed herself and then spent a few minutes writing the diary entry that she always composed before breakfast. It would have made more sense to write the entire entry for the day in the evening, when there would be more to say, but the morning entry had come to be a form of statement of intent, setting out what she hoped the day would bring. She wrote:

This morning, my mother is coming back from hospital in Kandy. She hurt her leg when she fell from the Pavilion in the Clouds. It is very steep below, and she could have fallen for a long way – maybe a mile, I'm not sure. But the trees saved her. Their branches stopped her going all the way to the bottom. That is probably because Jesus was watching and did not want her to die just yet. You only go to heaven when it is time for you to go. Before that time, lots of dangerous things can happen to you, and you will still be all right. Miss White says this is not true. She says that God and Jesus and the Holy Ghost have more important things to do than worry about what happens to us. I am not sure who is right about this.

I will be very good when my mother comes home. I will ask Michael to make her one of those cakes that she really likes. He does not mind making them as long as he does not have too many other things to cook. He has a bicycle that he rides up from the lines. He does not like the Hindu people, particularly those in the lower lines, because he says they fill their houses with idols. He says they are a very low-caste people and will not touch them, even if he is a Christian. He says that they do not know what a waste of time it is to put food out in front of the Hindu gods. He says that the dogs come along and eat the food, and then everybody says that it is a miracle and the food has been eaten by the gods. He says people are very foolish to believe things like that when there are many good miracles in the Bible if only they would look at them. But he says they won't because they are trapped in ignorance. Miss White also says that there are many people trapped in ignorance. She says that if you don't pay attention to your lessons you will be trapped in ignorance for the rest of your life.

I am not going to be trapped in ignorance because I shall be going off to school in Scotland quite soon. They have shown me a picture of one of the schools over there. They have a big gym where the girls can swing on ropes. They have a school orchestra that has violins and trumpets. I would like to learn the violin.

I am going to be staying with my aunt when I am at school. I have seen a photograph of her. She is quite tall and wears her hair in a bun. My mother says that that shows how clever she is. If you wear your hair in a bun you are probably very good at mathematics and history. My aunt has a house in a street. I am not sure what it will be like to live in a street. We live on a hill, which is different from a street.

I hope that my mother's leg gets better soon. Miss White says she may have to use crutches if her leg is really hurt. My father says he is not sure whether this is so. He says that sometimes you can use a stick to help you walk. He says it all depends.

Miss White likes my father. She has not got a husband herself as no man has ever asked her to marry him. You have to wait until a man asks you to marry him. You are not allowed to ask a man to marry you, as that is against the law. If nobody asks you to marry him then you are a spinster and have to live in a spinster's house. You are allowed to keep a dog or a cat, though.

Miss White says she knew plenty of men in Calcutta. She told me about them and how brave they were. One of them had shot a tiger, she said, and had made the tiger into a rug. I think that is unkind, as tigers never did anything to us, although sometimes they eat people who are not looking. That is probably your fault then, as you would not be eaten if you were keeping a look-out. Miss White says that tigers sometimes eat farmers in India when they make their fields on the edge of the jungle. She said that is a very dangerous thing to do. She says that there was a man who was eaten by a tiger and all that was left of him was his hat. She says that tigers very rarely eat hats, and, if they do, they spit them out.

I don't like Miss White all that much. She is all right, but not for the whole time. I think that she would like my mother to go away so that she could marry my father instead. He cannot ask her to marry him because he is already married, and it is against the law to marry two people at the same time. If you do, you go to jail for at least ten years, and all they give you to eat in jail is porridge. Sometimes they have bread and a bit of jam, but not very often. There is no pudding in jail.

I am glad that nobody will ever read this because I say things in my diary that I would not say to my best friend. When I get to Scotland, I shall have a best friend. I will choose somebody who is pretty and who is good at swinging on ropes in the gym. There will be lots of girls like that, and they will all be on the look-out for a best friend. I must go now, because I have to get ready for breakfast. I have not washed yet, but nobody will know.

It was agreed with Miss White that lessons could be suspended for a few days, so that Bella could spend more time with her mother. Virginia had been ordered to rest, confined to a day bed that had been set up on a screened-off section of the veranda, where it was cool, and where the screen provided protection from insects. A samovar had been placed on one of the brass-tray tables, and this, heated by a small spirit stove at its base, provided tea at regular intervals for the invalid or her guests. There was a good supply of newspapers and magazines, delivered by post to Colombo by the mail boat, and then sent up, along with the most recent books posted by the bookseller in Colombo. The members of the reading circle visited individually, dropping off yet more reading matter and bringing Virginia up to date on the latest gossip from the club in Nuwara Eliya. There had been talk about cheating having taken place in the club's bridge tournament, a devastating accusation for which there was no proof, but which, if established, would have destroyed, for all time, the reputation of the accused.

There were differing allegations as to the nature of the cheating. "They coughed a lot," said one of the ladies. "I tell you, it was like a Swiss sanitorium. Two hearts, *cough, cough*; two spades, *cough, cough, cough*."

Another said that the offenders had adjusted their wedding rings as a way of signalling their holding. "They could indicate exactly how many cards they had of a particular suit by turning the ring round," she said. "They were fiendishly clever."

And another said that the way in which the secret messages were conveyed was through lip reading. "He didn't actually say anything," she said. "But she was an expert lip-reader and could tell from the movement of the lips. I have that on good authority, you know."

Virginia knew the couple concerned. She doubted all of this, although she was as keen as anybody to hear the details.

"I don't think they'd manage any of that," she said. "And I think they're innocent. He has no memory for what cards go out – he can barely count trumps. She plays the first card that comes into her head." She smiled as she recollected a litany of careless revokes. "But they sometimes get away with it. There's a divinity that hedges bridge players like them."

This brought disappointment, and the conversation switched, reluctantly, to the news from home. "I think Chamberlain's doing his best," said one of the ladies. "He's the only one who can deal with that man."

Another disagreed. "They're dead set on causing trouble. Dead set."

"Well, at least we're far enough away. They can't do much out here."

"The whole world is topsy-turvy."

"They say the Pope doesn't like Mussolini – and who can blame him?"

Virginia listened to all this. It kept her entertained, although she disagreed with much of what was said. For calmer conversation, she turned to Bella, to whom she would read from Palgrave or *A Hundred and Seventy Chinese Poems*. They listened to music together, with Bella winding up the Gilbert gramophone, changing the metal needles, and putting the records on the turntable. Virginia liked Beniamino Gigli and had a full set of *Lucia di Lammermoor*. Bella suffered through that but was dutiful in operating the gramophone; she preferred *The Mikado*. Miss White had a gramophone too. Sometimes both were played at the same time, competing against one another like two opposing military bands assembled on the same battlefield.

Virginia said, "I feel so useless, lying here. But I suppose I'm lucky." She looked at her Bella. "You should always remember how lucky you are."

"I am," said Bella. "I have lots of nice things in my life."

Virginia sighed. "I would love to be able to conjure up more company for you. Some girls for you to play with." She sighed again. "But you know how it is. And you have your dolls, of course – they've been marvellous."

Bella reached out to touch Li Po and Po Chü-i, who were sitting beside her on the chair. "Li Po has got a very good brain," she said. "Most of his head is brain, you know."

"I can well believe it."

There was a brief silence. "He says some strange things, though. Not always – just sometimes."

Virginia reached for a magazine that had been left by one of the visiting ladies. *The Illustrated London News*. There was a picture of the launch of a liner. "Such a waste of champagne," she muttered.

"Li Po was wondering how the barrier gave way. He thinks it very odd."

Virginia was reading the account of the launch. There was information about the number of cabins, and there was a picture of the first-class accommodation. Was it worth it – paying all that money for a few weeks of comfort? Of course, you would have more fresh water for your bath – that counted for something. They gave you so little in the cheaper cabins. She was only half listening to what her daughter was saying, but then Bella said, "Li Po says he thinks it was Miss White."

The top of *The Illustrated London News* quivered. Then it was lowered. "Miss White?"

"Yes. He says – that's Li Po – he says he saw her going into the Pavilion. He said he saw her doing something to the barrier."

A trapped fly buzzed against the screen. Otherwise, there was silence.

"Li Po said that?"

"Yes."

"But darling, Li Po is a dolly. He doesn't speak."

"That's what you think. Li Po speaks all the time. Po Chü-i speaks too, but not so much. He has a very funny voice – like the way people speak when they've been given laughing gas."

Virginia smiled. "I don't think you should believe everything Li Po says. You know what dollies are like – they make things up. Some of them are terrible fibbers. Look at Pinocchio – he was the biggest fibber of them all, and he was a dolly. His nose grew longer if he told a fib – you've heard that story. Li Po doesn't have much of a nose, of course, but all the same . . ."

"But he's right. I saw her go in there. I saw her with my own eyes."

Virginia placed *The Illustrated London News* back on the pile. She spoke gently, as one might speak to a nervous witness. "You saw her? You did?"

Bella's tone was matter-of-fact. "Yes. I saw her that day. It was just getting dark. Or not quite. I could still see everything. Li Po and Po Chü-i were sitting on the windowsill." She gave her mother a challenging look. "Ask them, if you don't believe me. And I looked out and saw Miss White walking across the lawn. She went into the Pavilion. She really did. I saw her. She went right up to the barrier. I think she did something to it."

For a few moments Virginia said nothing. Then, "You aren't making this up, are you, darling?"

Bella shook her head. "Why would I make it up?"

"Because . . . well, sometimes people make things up because they think that what really happened is too boring. It's like making up a fairy story."

She looked at her mother resentfully. "I told you I didn't. I told you I saw her. And Li Po and Po Chü-i saw her too. They see everything."

Virginia looked at her watch. Henry came back from the tea office every day at one, for his lunch. He would be back in fifteen minutes.

"I think you should go and have your lunch now," she said. "Daddy and I need to talk. We'll have our lunch a bit later."

Bella picked up the two dolls and tucked them under her arm. They did not mind the indignity – they were used to it. I am not a fibber, she thought. I *did* see Miss White going into the Pavilion. I didn't see what she did there, but she probably did do something to the barrier. Why else would she have gone in there? Miss White was wicked. She was a wicked person pretending to be a governess. She had been in prison in Calcutta – for being a witch, probably – and had run away to Ceylon to get away from the police. She had her plans all along, of course, and that was to get rid of the person who could stop her from marrying her father. It was a wicked plan, and she had almost pulled it off. But she did not know that three sets of eyes were watching her every move: hers, Li Po's and Po Chü-i's. They had seen what she was up to.

Henry came back from the office buoyed by news of the imminent arrival of a new piece of machinery for the factory. A replacement for an old dryer had arrived in Colombo and would be sent up the following week if the roads were clear. It would be far more efficient, he said, and could increase the factory's output considerably. They were already processing the surplus harvest of a number of their smaller neighbours and could take on more after the new machine had been installed.

He realised that Virginia was not paying attention.

"Something on your mind?" he asked. "Leg bothering you?"

"It's not my leg," she said. "It's hardly hurting at all now. It's . . ."

She broke off. He frowned, and sat down beside her day bed.

"Are you feeling a bit low?" he asked, and then, before she had time to reply, he continued, "I don't blame you if you are. That's a nasty thing that happened." He shook his head in self-reproach. "I feel responsible for it, you know. I try to keep an eye on this place, and I shouldn't have missed something like that."

She brushed aside his regrets. "It's not your fault at all – not in the slightest. No, that's not what's been worrying me."

He waited for her to continue. "There's something else?"

She hesitated before continuing. "Bella was talking to me."

"Oh yes?"

"She's having her lunch by herself. I said I wanted to speak to you before we had ours."

He seemed to relax now. Taking a handkerchief out of his pocket, he mopped his brow. "It's warmer than usual today." He looked up at the slow-moving ceiling fan that had recently been installed in that part of the veranda – a modern addition to the natural air conditioning of altitude. He had not been sure that it would make much difference – "These things just stir up the air, when all's said and done" – but now he offered to turn it on.

She shook her head. "I'm perfectly comfortable. Not moving even makes one feel a bit too cool."

"I've been in the factory. That's always a bit on the warm side."

He noticed that she was not looking at him directly but was gazing out over the lawn, out past the line of trees that marked the edge of the garden on that side. The fall of the land in that direction was less sudden than on the Pavilion side, and a winding path had been constructed that led down to the edge of the tea gardens. The pickers sometimes used that when they were working in that particular section, and they would occasionally see a short line of women skirting the lawn to take the shortcut. "I can tell them not to use that path," he had said. But Virginia did not mind. "Don't make their job any harder," she said. She felt guilty – she always had. They paid these people so little. They were so well-off themselves. Fate could reverse these things.

"So what did Bella have to say?"

She suddenly wanted to do something with her hands. She picked up the previously discarded copy of *The Illustrated London News*. His eyes followed her hands.

"Those dolls of hers . . ."

A smile played about his lips. There had been some residual tension, and now it seemed dispelled. This was a matter about dolls; this was nothing important.

"The Chinese poets?" he said. "Li what's-his-name and Cho something-or-other . . ."

"Li Po and Po Chü-i. Yes."

He had been carrying a light tropical jacket with him. He rarely wore it, but he took it with him to the office each morning as one might take a briefcase, as part of a uniform. One never knew what visitors might turn up unannounced – buyers from Colombo, or insurance people, or officials of one sort or another. The jacket might be donned for their benefit. Now he reached in its pocket and took out a flat pack of cigarettes. He did not smoke very much, but occasionally he lit up, as he did now. She disliked smoking; her father had a smoker's cough, and that had always worried her. Smoking didn't help.

"You don't mind, do you?" he asked, as he lit the cigarette.

She shook her head. She understood why so many smokers found smoking settled them: it gave them something to do with their hands. We needed to do something with our hands – hence handbags and worry beads and rings that could be twisted around fingers to give forbidden signals at bridge . . .

"Bella thinks the dolls can speak. She seems convinced of it."

He laughed, and the smoke came out of his mouth in a brief translucent cloud. "Children have their notions, don't they? They're imaginative little creatures. Fairies and so on – they believe in them, don't they? They actually think there are fairies." He paused. "Mind you, there were those otherwise reasonable people who believed those ridiculous photographs. Remember? Conan Doyle himself was taken in. They believed those photographs of fairies. And they were adults."

He drew again on his cigarette, frowning as he did so. "And that's before one even thinks of the Hindus and all those gods of theirs." He gestured down the hill, in the direction of what they called the *distant lines,* the rows of houses, not much more than hovels, where the least skilled Tamil workers lived, the *pariahs* – houses bursting at the seams with uncles and aunts and countless children, all dependent on a single wage. "They believe in them, I suppose. Ganesh and so on. An elephant with hands – I ask you! And Lord Hanuman – a monkey god . . . Talking dolls don't seem so strange if you sign up to any of that."

She lowered her eyes, embarrassed at the sacrilege, although there was nobody else to witness it. Did they themselves not believe in things that were every bit as fanciful? A virgin birth? Shepherds and stars? Angels – serried ranks of them? She did not like the thought of mocking the spirituality of people who were at the bottom of the insidious and incorrigible caste system, who were considered polluters, who did not know how to read – because nobody had bothered to teach them. And yet she was loyal to her husband, for all his male assumptions: he did not ordain any of the social architecture that placed them *here* and so many unfortunate others *there*. None of that was his doing.

Now she struggled to bring the conversation back to the lines she had intended. "She said that the dolls saw something."

He rolled his eyes. "Well, I imagine that if they can talk, then they presumably should be able to see things."

He was amused – she could see that – but suddenly his demeanour changed. It was anxiety. He was worried. She saw it clearly – written on him – written on the way he held the cigarette, in the angle of his head, in the way he suddenly touched the lobe of his right ear. He did that when he was worried; she had observed it many times.

A cold hand touched at her. She felt it. He was worried because there was something for the dolls to see. But it was too late to stop, and she continued, "Bella said that Li Po and Po Chü-i saw Miss White going into the Pavilion."

For a few moments he said nothing. But then, before he replied, she saw his anxiety evaporate.

"Well," he said, his voice quite even, "that's hardly surprising. She's free to use the garden, and we've never asked her to keep away from the Pavilion." He broke off.

"Except, I suppose, when you have your reading-circle ladies here. I've noticed that you don't include her."

There was a note of reproach in his voice. She looked away. "I have to have something of my own."

He was placatory. "Of course you do. I didn't mean that as a criticism. It was just an observation."

She hesitated, but then, "The point is this: she said that the dolls had seen her going in there shortly before I did."

"When?"

"On the day. On the day this happened." She gestured towards her bandage.

He waited.

"She said that she was at the barrier – the fence, whatever you call it. The bit that gave way."

He seemed puzzled. "Lavender?"

That was the governess's name: Lavender. But he never called her that, and neither did Virginia. Nobody was called Lavender any more. She was Miss White.

He seemed to realise his mistake. "Miss White was at the barrier . . . in the Pavilion? Is that what you're saying?"

"Not me. The dolls said it . . . Oh, for goodness' sake, the dolls said nothing. Bella did."

"Of course. But why would Bella say that?"

"She said that she saw it herself. She said something about seeing it with her own eyes."

He looked for an ashtray but, seeing none, stubbed out his cigarette on the sole of his shoe before depositing it in the saucer of a teacup.

"I wish you wouldn't do that, Henry. I really do."

He grinned like a schoolboy caught *in flagrante*. "Sorry, but what can a chap do? If I threw it in the flower bed, I'd get it in the neck – spoiling the cannas, or whatever."

Rather to her surprise, his levity reassured her. A man

who had something to hide would not talk like this, but would be . . . she had to search for the word before it came to her: would be *furtive*.

"I don't know what to make of it," she said. "You said – if I remember correctly – you said that Miss White said . . ."

He interrupted her. "That sounds a bit complicated: *you said that she said* . . ."

"But you did. You said that she told you that she had been in her bungalow all afternoon. You said she claimed not to have gone out to the Pavilion until after it happened – when she went with you and Michael." She paused. "That's what you told me, isn't it?"

He shrugged. "I can't really remember. Perhaps I did. I was in a bit of a state, of course – I still am, to tell you the truth. This has been a bit of a shock to the system."

Now his demeanour changed. The lightness left, and he reached out to touch her arm gently, in a gesture of concern. "I'm not sure that you should be bothering yourself over all this. Is it important?"

She sighed. "I don't know – I really don't know. It's just that Bella has come up with this rather odd comment, and, frankly, I don't know what to make of it."

He became decisive. "If I were you, I'd forget about it. Children are imaginative little creatures. Talking dolls and so on. For all we know, she has some sort of grudge against Miss White and is having a go at her."

Virginia considered this. "By trying to get her into trouble? By making us think she was somehow responsible for my fall? Is that what you're suggesting?"

"Not suggesting. I don't think that it's necessarily what's happening – but it could be, don't you think?"

She was not sure what to think. Bella was a truthful child – or had been up until now. When confronted with some bit of wrongdoing, some failure to do what she had been asked to do, she tended to own up rather than deny. And even her invention of the talking dolls was an open one – shared with anybody who cared to listen. That was unusual – many children were secretive about their private worlds. Many had imaginary friends whom their parents never met. Bella was not like that: Li Po and Po Chü-i were out in the open, there for anybody to see.

"I don't know what to think," said Virginia. "Have you looked at the barrier? I've been assuming that the wood was rotten. Have you found anything that points to . . ."

He waited.

". . . to another explanation?" she continued.

He smiled. "Darling, the last thing in the world that I expect is *another explanation,* as you so tactfully put it. No, I've had a look, and I got the carpenter to do so too. You remember him? That man with the scar on his chin? He's one of the Lankan Tamils, and he's pretty genned up on anything to do with wood. Not surprisingly. Anyway, he looked, and he said that one of the spars was a bit suspect. He said that if water gets in around a bolt or a nail it can result in weakness. He said that's probably what happened."

"I see." She was relieved. She did not want to believe otherwise.

"Anyway, he's already fixed it. He's going to paint the new section to match the rest of the Pavilion. He does a very good job, usually." He paused, straightening the crease in his trousers before he stood up. "I asked him to look at the struts below – you know, the beams that keep the Pavilion in position. They go into concrete that's been put in the rock immediately below – on the cliff face, if you see what I mean. He's done that now. His men lowered him on a rope – there was an awful lot of shouting of instructions. I told them that they were not to drop him, and that led to a lot more shouting, I can tell you. I told them they'd have their pay docked if they dropped the carpenter."

She smiled weakly. "And?"

"And he gave everything a clean bill of health."

He rose to his feet.

"I think we should have lunch. Michael has made lamb chops, I believe."

She took his extended hand and got gingerly to her feet. "Goat. He calls goat lamb."

"What's the expression? Mutton dressed as lamb?"

She laughed. "Yes. I heard somebody use that in the club the other day. They referred to Mrs Wilson – you know her – that rather forbidding-looking woman who's on the social committee – they referred to her as mutton dressed as lamb."

"And is she?"

"I'm afraid she is."

He smiled. "We all have our faults. Even the best of us. Our strengths and our weaknesses."

She thought: *weaknesses*. But she said nothing and took his arm as he led her into the dining room, where the goat dressed as lamb would soon be put before them, along with over-boiled potatoes and spinach to which Michael would have added far too much grated nutmeg.

5

Just the Way It Is

From her vantage point on the veranda, Virginia watched the pair of Ceylon green pigeons preening each other on their favourite branch. They were creatures of habit, these birds, and this couple were regular mid-morning visitors to one of the trees bordering the lawn. She was not particularly interested in the bird life of the surrounding forest and felt embarrassed when a visitor asked her the name of some bird. "Heaven knows," she would reply. "I suspect even the bird is not quite sure what it's called." This usually brought a smile on the visitor's part and on her part a resolution, never carried out, to learn something of the bird life of the island. After all, this was where she belonged, even if she had spent those long years of schooling back home, and would end up there, she suspected, at some vague point in a future of reminiscence and struggle against encroaching cold. She had been aware of such people – some of them relatives – who inhabited villas on the outskirts of places like Dundee after lives spent on the banks of the Hooghly or in some other spot of a rambling and outrageous empire. She would join them in her turn, she feared, with her albums of black-and-white photographs, wooden carvings of water buffalos and Buddhas, remembering a more colourful, more passionate life somewhere far away. But the future is always hypothetical for those under a certain age – the age at which the penny of realisation drops – and for the present there was plenty of time to put off such projects as learning the names of the local birds or identifying the trees and shrubs populating the surrounding slopes.

Her conversation with Henry had taken place the previous day, and she had had an afternoon and evening to think about it. She had thought of little else and had, as a result, been too distracted to read, other than to page through magazines she had already perused several times. What concerned her most was Henry's body language: his normal manner was relaxed, and she could always tell, from a certain tenseness in his expression and in his posture, if he was on edge about something. There had been a defensiveness about his manner that had crept into his tone of voice. It had been as if he was expecting an accusation of some sort and was readying himself to rebuff it. It had been unmistakable.

And yet there was a perfectly innocent explanation for this. Henry himself had said that he felt guilty about her fall – that it had happened at all was an implicit reproach to his attentiveness. Nature here was not benign: there were all sorts of dangers that had to be guarded against, ranging from the minor irritation of biting insects to the potential catastrophe of a snake bite. There were flash floods, there were lightning storms, there was the ever-present threat of rabies in both wild and domestic animals. The attention of the pi-dogs frequenting the outskirts of villages was potentially fatal, as might be the almost undetectable nip of a fruit bat. Stories abounded throughout the country of people who had ignored a dog bite, or even the lick of an unknown dog, developed hydrophobia and gone on to die an agonising death. "If that ever happens to me," Henry had said, only half jokingly, "I'd like you to take a gun to me right at the beginning. Don't make me go through all those stages." It would not be murder, he said – it would be mercy killing, which was something quite different.

Henry had always been the one to protect her from such things, and yet on his watch, within sight of the house itself, she had almost plunged to her death. It was only natural that he should feel guilty about that and that this guilt should translate itself into a tense manner. And yet it seemed to her that there something more than this at play here. Henry was not telling her the truth: that was what she picked up. You could always tell if people close to you were lying: it was almost impossible for them to dissemble in the way in which a stranger might do.

But what was he seeking to conceal? Her greatest concern was that he and Miss White were having an affair. It was the stuff of a thousand stories: into a household comes a stranger whose very presence threatens an otherwise stable marriage. And who better to exert that baneful influence but a governess? Men were weak – everybody knew that – and they grew tired of the inevitable monotony of married life. Henry seemed happy enough, but that did not mean that he might not be enticed by the thought of an occasional adventure. The club was full of such stories, most of which had no dramatic denouement but fizzled out in time, with everybody returning to their old routines. Very rarely, a wife or a husband would go off with a lover and never be heard from again, but that had not happened for a long time. Henry was not one to go anywhere very much: he was too involved in the estate to abandon it. "We have eight hundred people dependent on this business," he said to her one evening. "Eight hundred, if you count the children and grandparents and the various hangers-on. Then there are the nurses. The teachers. The sweepers. Not to forget the priests and the astrologers." He looked at her, as if for support, and she made a gesture of acceptance with her hands.

"That's just the way it is," she said.

"Yes," he said, simply. "I suppose that's so. Just the way it is."

He had not intended to mention the priests, but they were on his mind. There were two of them, theirs and one on a neighbouring estate. The priest on the neighbouring estate had a reputation as an astrologer and was much in demand for casting wedding horoscopes. One of the men in the factory, a Buddhist electrician who had no use for Hindu priests, had told Henry, in a confidential aside, that the priest had cast a horoscope that suggested the Japanese would come and would kill him.

He looked at the electrician open-mouthed. "Me? The Japanese?"

The electrician lowered his eyes. He was clearly embarrassed. "I only tell you so that you should be careful," he said.

"But you don't pay any attention to that nonsense, do you?"

The electrician hesitated. But then he remembered he was a Christian, and so he said, "It is all first-class rubbish."

"Exactly, Mr Gunawardena – first-class rubbish is precisely what it is."

Henry had made light of it, but it had unnerved him. These priests are a nuisance, he thought: they make it difficult for anybody to do anything without taking the auspices – and paying for them. If he could, he would show them the door – ban them from the estate, with all their fakirs' tricks – but there would be a labour revolt if he did that. So he left them to work their spells and magic, their elaborate purification rituals, their mumbo jumbo, as he thought of it. And he would not tell Virginia about what had been said. It was beyond ridiculous.

Now, as she lay on her day bed, her leg propped up with a pillow as Dr Pereira had recommended, she watched the two pigeons in their cooing solicitation – a perfect allegory for matrimonial bliss. But their example seemed only to underline her discomfort and to remind her of the course of action she had first thought about earlier that morning and that now seemed to her to be inevitable.

The house was silent. Henry had left shortly after breakfast to supervise the final drying of a large batch of leaf. It was a process that he liked to attend to in person, as there were delicate decisions to be made as to the point at which drying was stopped. The misjudgement of the moment could spoil the taste of the tea, making it bitter, as had happened a few weeks ago. It was an expensive mistake, and he did not want it repeated. Bella was on Miss White's veranda, working with the governess on her arithmetic, a subject she enjoyed. She had Li Po and Po Chü-i with her, seated on a shoe box, allowed to attend the lesson on condition of non-interference. Li Po, she said, was good at figures, while Po Chü-i struggled with even the simplest sums. "He's good at other things," she said. "He knows a lot about history." Miss White listened to this but simply rolled her eyes.

There was a house servant, who moved from room to room sweeping and tidying, but he was dealing with the washing in the small laundry block behind the bungalow. He was adept with the iron, heated by small lumps of glowing charcoal, and in due course would deliver piles of smartly pressed sheets and clothing, but it would take up most of the morning. So the only person in the house, apart from

Virginia, was Michael. He was mixing bread dough in the kitchen, dusting his hands with flour to allow him to feel the dough into just the right consistency.

She had a small brass bell, of the sort imported from the foundries of India. It was decorated with monkeys in relief around the rim, the handle formed by the curling tail of one of them. She picked this up and rang it firmly.

Michael appeared after a couple of minutes, wearing his apron and wiping flour off his hands.

"I see you're making bread," said Virginia.

Michael nodded. "I am making two loaves. Big ones. Then I will make soup for your lunch. I have some chicken."

Virginia fiddled with the bell. He watched her. "Good. I like chicken soup. Don't put any peppers in it. I don't like it if it's spicy."

"I will not," he said.

She waited for a few moments. She put down the bell and then smoothed the surface of the pillow under her injured leg. "Where is Nikku?"

"He is doing laundry, Lady."

"I'd like you to fetch somebody for me, Michael."

He waited. The flour was off his hands now, but he still rubbed them gently.

"You know the carpenter? The head carpenter?"

Michael inclined his head. "The very fat man?"

She smiled. "He enjoys his food, I think. Yes, that man. Can you fetch him from his workshop? You know the place?"

Michael did. "I can fetch him."

He began to leave, but she stopped him. "No, wait a moment. I want you to fetch him without anybody knowing. I want to talk to him privately."

Michael looked confused. "It is light. People will see me . . ."

"No, that's all right. I just don't want to bother my husband about this."

He said nothing, but she saw that he bit his lip.

"It's not important," she said quickly. "I just want to ask this man something. And I want you to be here to interpret. I don't think he has very good English."

He waited for further instruction, but she indicated by a movement of her hand that he should set off on his errand. After he had gone, she reached for *The Illustrated London News* and began to page through it. The duchess was still launching her ship, the bottle of champagne swinging through the air on its brief journey. She examined the photograph, studying the woman's outfit and the fashionable people standing around her. She felt a pang of resentment, of envy, over a world that she was cut off from, here on this distant hillside where nothing happened. She turned the page. Italian troops were pictured in a village in Abyssinia. They were smiling. In the background, two small boys, holding hands, were staring at them with the frank, unblinking curiosity of childhood. And there was Mussolini in Rome, visiting a hospital, escorted by nuns wearing wimples topped with twin peaks. The nuns were smiling at Mussolini. *The brute*, she thought. The brutes were taking over the world: nuns seemed not to understand that.

It did not take Michael long to complete his errand. Announcing his presence with a knock on the door leading off into the corridor, he brought the carpenter onto the veranda. Virginia indicated a chair, and the man lowered himself onto it. The chair squeaked in protest at his weight, and Virginia thought, *Well, at least if he breaks it, he'll know how to fix it.* She glanced at Michael. "Tell him we can speak in Tamil if he likes."

Michael explained, and the man nodded his assent. He looked anxious.

"I just wanted to ask you about our pavilion," she began. "That's all."

Michael translated, and the man relaxed. He had been gripping his hat in his hands; now he stopped kneading the brim.

"You told my husband that the wood on the barrier there was rotten. You said that's why it gave way."

The translation was made. The man nodded.

Michael translated his reply. "He says that he's very sorry that you fell. He said that it was very good fortune that you landed in a tree."

"Tell him thank you."

This was done. Then Virginia said, "So the wood was rotten?"

Michael spoke quickly. The carpenter shook his head and gave a lengthy reply.

"He says he did not say it was rotten," Michael said. "He said that he told Mr Henry that there was nothing wrong with it."

Virginia frowned. "No rotten wood?"

The carpenter understood this without the translation. He shook his head. He switched to English. "Wood good. The wood is good. Very good wood."

Virginia did not say anything for a few moments. Then, "But what happened?"

The man launched into a torrent of Tamil. After a couple of minutes, Michael reached out and tapped him on the arm to stop him.

"This man," Michael began, "says that he does not

know what happened. He says that sometimes things happen for no reason. He says that they just happen. He says it is like that."

Virginia looked at Michael. "Ask him this: is he sure that he did not say anything about rotten wood? Is he one hundred per cent sure?"

Words were exchanged.

"One hundred per cent," said Michael at last. "He says that he is telling the truth."

"Thank him – from me. Tell him that it is best if he doesn't discuss this with anybody. Tell him that I mean that. There'll be trouble if he talks to anybody about it. Make sure he understands that."

Michael explained, and the man nodded. He arose from the chair, which creaked once more. Virginia looked away, over towards the pavilion, which she could not quite see, and by the time she looked back, they had gone. People moved quietly here, she thought. Like shadows.

6

The Illustrated London News

They were sitting in the schoolroom at the back of the bungalow. It was the dreariest room in the house, a converted storeroom with brown linoleum floors and skirting boards of the same colour. An attempt had been made to brighten the walls with a display of maps and cut-out pictures of children in their schoolrooms in various parts of the world. The children, scrubbed for the camera, sat alert at their desks under an African tree; three small Eskimo children, their faces framed in fur hoods, were improbably posed, books on knees, in a large igloo; two attentive Australian children huddled, beaming, about a radio on a sheep-station veranda. All of them, Bella felt, were better placed than she was – particularly the Australian boy and girl with their school-of-the-air; she would far prefer a radio set to Miss White, she thought.

They were working their way through a page of arithmetic exercises, having spent an initial half hour on multiplication tables. Bella was good at those, including the thirteen-times table, which even her mother, she discovered, was hazy about. "We never got quite that far," said Virginia. "In my day it wasn't quite so important. There were other things you had to know."

Bella was curious. "Such as?"

"Kings and queens. Alfred and the cakes. King Canute. Robert the Bruce and the spider. The Amazon. Oh, there was a lot."

"I'll never know all those things."

Virginia told her not to be defeatist. "You pick things up as you go along. Once you get to school – to a proper school – you'll learn an awful lot."

But now Miss White was on to the ancient issue of the men digging a ditch and the timing of their labours. "Now listen carefully," she said. "If it takes two men one hour to dig a ditch, then how long will it take one man?"

She thought for a while. It depended, surely, on how quickly that man would dig. Some people were slow – she had seen them digging the ditches at the side of the road: they leaned on their shovels and smoked; they only really worked when the supervisor came along on his bicycle and berated them. It would take ten such men to dig a ditch in an hour.

"One hour and fifteen minutes," she said.

Miss White sucked in her cheeks. That was always a sign that an answer was wrong.

Bella corrected herself. "One and a half hours," she said. "Or maybe three hours if they're lazy."

Miss White looked disapproving. "No," she said firmly. "It's nothing to do with what the men are like. Let us assume for the moment that the men all work at the same rate. They're all the same sort of man."

"Are they Tamils?"

Miss White smiled. "That's neither here nor there. They could be Tamil, or they could be Buddhist. They could be Mohammedans, or even Parsis, for that matter, but perhaps not them. No, perhaps not Parsis."

Bella did not know what a Parsi was. "You would be unlikely to find Parsis digging ditches," Miss White said. "They are a very cultivated people. They usually do skilled work. They're businessmen and accountants. Engineers. That sort of thing. They have very characteristic names."

"Such as?'

"Any name with *wala* in it is likely to be a Parsi name. I met a Mr Bankwala in Calcutta. His people had worked in a bank. And there are families called Cakewala."

"Who made cakes?"

"Yes, but we are meant to be doing arithmetic. Think again: two men dig the ditch in an hour – will one man take a longer or a shorter time?"

Bella was confident enough about that. "Longer – because he won't have anybody to help him."

"Yes, that's right. But how much longer?"

Bella looked at Li Po and Po Chü-i, who were seated at the top of her desk, propped up against one another. They did not attend all of Miss White's lessons but appeared at some. They did not like arithmetic.

"Does it matter how long it takes to dig a ditch?" asked Li Po.

Bella had to explain to him that this was not a real ditch. "This is just pretend. All arithmetic is just pretend."

Li Po thought that there was no point in wasting one's time on pretend things. Po Chü-i agreed, although he normally agreed with everything that Li Po said.

"How deep is this ditch?" asked Li Po.

"She didn't say," replied Bella. "I don't think she knows."

Miss White had written something on the schoolroom's small blackboard. 2 MEN TAKE 1 HOUR – 1 MAN TAKES 2x1 = 2 HOURS. She turned and looked at Bella.

"What are you muttering, Bella?"

Bella did not reply. Li Po was saying something about long division.

"Are you paying attention?" snapped Miss White.

Bella did not hear her. Li Po had confessed that he found long division hard. Po Chü-i agreed. "I'll never learn it," he said. "Never."

"You mustn't give up," said Bella. "It doesn't matter if you're not very good at something – you have to keep trying."

Miss White drew in her breath. "Bella, I don't know what you're thinking, but I've had enough of these wretched dolls. If you can't keep your mind on your lessons, those dolls are going to have to stay outside." She paused. "Are you listening to what I'm saying?'

She was not. Li Po was saying something about his breakfast. He liked kedgeree. All dolls like kedgeree.

Miss White moved across the room. Standing over Bella's desk, she reached for Li Po. "This has gone far enough," she said. "These dolls are a distraction. You're letting your imagination run away with you. This is a schoolroom – not a playroom. And you, young lady, are eight – soon to be nine. You're not a little girl any longer."

She picked up Li Po. "Li Po can wait outside the door," she said. "And Po Chü-i too, while we're about it."

Bella snatched at Li Po. "No, Miss White, you mustn't. They'll stop talking – I promise."

Miss White was holding Li Po by his right arm – pencil-thin – a tiny stuffed tube of material at the bottom of which was a minute hand, the fingers delineated by delicate stitching – not much of an arm, but all that Li Po had. Bella had grasped him by his legs, covered, for the most part, by an ankle-length silk mandarin coat, the coat that a Chinese poet would have worn on an important day – a day on which visitors might arrive at the river jetty.

Miss White pulled, as did Bella, and Li Po was for a brief moment a distended rag doll tugged in two different directions. Then his arm came off, the stitches connecting it to his body giving way in a series of tiny ruptures. Out of the arm came the living flesh, white horsehair, tightly rolled. Bella let out an involuntary scream: "Li Po! His arm . . ."

Miss White stared at the tiny detached arm. For a few moments she said nothing, and then, handing the arm back to Bella, she said, "I'm very sorry. I didn't mean to damage it."

The apology added insult. *It*. He was not a *thing*; he was Li Po.

Miss White reached for the rest of Li Po. "Let me look," she said. "Let me see what I can do."

Bella nursed the broken body of the doll. She began to sob.

Miss White looked pained. "I'm so sorry. It really was an accident, Bella." She prised the doll out of Bella's hands. "Look, the body isn't torn. It's just the arm that's come off."

Just the arm that's come off . . . thought Bella. *Would a doctor say that about a person? It's just your arm that's come off . . .*

She waited for Li Po to say something, but he was in shock. All that could be heard was a keening sound from Po Chü-i, who had witnessed the incident at close quarters. She shouldn't have allowed Miss White to hold him – not now, in his injured state. She would be unable to hear anything he said, because only Bella could hear what the dolls said. Adults did not understand – how could they?

"I tell you what we should do," said Miss White. "Why don't we go straight to my bungalow? I have needle and thread there, and I'm sure we'll find a thread that matches the original. You won't notice a thing. It will be as good as new."

She immediately thought of Po Chü-i. "Po Chü-i will have to come as well. Li Po will need him. Please let me bring him."

Miss White pursed her lips. Guilt kept her from dismissing this request. "Bring them both, if you must." She paused. "And I really am terribly sorry, Bella. I know how much you love your dollies."

She closed her eyes in an effort to get control of herself. She should not take out her frustration on this little girl and her funny little dolls. It was not her fault that she did not want to think about how long it would take two men to dig a ditch. And it was always *men* . . . Did women not dig ditches? The answer, of course, was no, they did not. She had never seen a woman digging a ditch. But that was not because women could not dig ditches – clearly they could, and there must be places where they were digging ditches – there simply must be. They picked tea, and they weeded the tea gardens, but ditches were different. It was probably because men took all the ditch-digging jobs while women had to stay at home and perform tasks of domestic drudgery. If it took one woman ten minutes to change a baby, then how long would it take two women to change three babies? Or, more to the point, how long would it take one *man* to change one baby? A lot longer than ten minutes, she imagined, because he would spend fifteen minutes looking around for a woman to pass the baby onto to be changed. You had to laugh. You had to.

She did not particularly like her job. She had never imagined that she would end up being a governess – of all things. It was so Victorian in its sound. It was what you became if you were not of a class to be a domestic servant and if there was little immediate chance of getting married. You were not even a proper teacher, because you had none of the qualifications of a teacher. You became a governess because there was nothing else that you could reasonably do unless you were prepared to work in a shop or be a secretary. It was so unfair; it was so wrong, and it was all because you were a woman and were denied the opportunities that men took for their right. It made your blood boil – it truly did. And if you showed an interest in being what you really should be – a woman of intellect, with an interest in those things of the mind that men took for *their* preserve – then they called you a bluestocking.

At least in Calcutta there had been people who could talk about something, people who could hold their own with those back home in places like St Andrews and Cambridge. Whereas here there were the planters and their club and *The Illustrated London News* to read, and out-of-date copies of *The Times*, and talk about the same things day after day – about the next trip home and the letters that the children wrote from school and the difficulties of getting supplies of the things you needed and the sense that life was slipping away. Nobody talked about any of the things that mattered: about how science was going to change the way we lived and how psychologists were going to help us to overcome human evil, and about how the Russians were experimenting with a social system that would make war and poverty and competition a thing of the past. There were people talking about those very things, there were people writing poems about them – clever poems – but nobody here knew anything about that.

A *reading circle* . . . Who did they think they were? Bloomsbury? Virginia Woolf? And they had not invited her to a single meeting – not one – although they knew, right at the beginning, that she was there in her bungalow, a few yards away from the Pavilion in the Clouds, and it would not have been an effort for somebody to come over and say, *Would you care to join us, because we're discussing Mr D.H. Lawrence and we wondered if you might have something to add?* That would not have been too hard for them, and yet they did not do it because they knew that if she did join them, they might discover how little they knew about anything, and they did not want to find that out. It would be too depressing for words to have to be *them* with their tennis parties *and* at the same time to come to the realisation that you knew nothing about Mr D.H. Lawrence or Sidney and Beatrice Webb, or any of the people who were actually thinking about things.

She sighed. "Is that all right then? Should we go and fix this little tear? And I'll make you a cup of hot chocolate, and you can have one of my special barley sugars – how about that? Would that help – because I really am terribly sorry about your dolly's arm, Bella. I really am. Look at me. Just look at me. You can see that I'm sorry, can't you?"

A reluctant glance was followed by the faintest of nods.

"And Li Po will forgive me, I hope."

The question remained unanswered, hanging in the air like one of the clouds that moved across the hillside, wispy, drifting, as capable of lifting as of lingering and building up into a larger cloud altogether.

The following day Virginia declared that her period of recuperation was over. "It's better for me to be up and about," she said. "I have a few scratches here and there, but there's nothing wrong with me otherwise."

She insisted she was fit enough to use the car and drove over to the Macmillan bungalow so that Bella might say goodbye to Richard, who would be leaving for school in a few weeks' time.

"Richard is a very lucky boy," said Virginia. "He's starting off at a school in Dumfriesshire, which has a very strong rugby team. You know how he's always wanted to play rugby – well, now he'll get very good coaching. And lots of art, too. His mother was telling me the art teacher in the school has actually had an exhibition in Dumfries – and sold some of his paintings."

The car slowed down. A small group of women and children were crossing the road ahead, making their way up the hill. One of the children stumbled and had to be picked up by a woman in a red sari. The woman glanced apologetically in the direction of the car; the child's face was contorted in rage.

"Poor little thing," said Virginia. "Just a tiny tot, and a long walk, I imagine."

Li Po was sitting on Bella's lap. He could not look out of the window, but he could see the sky through the windscreen. His repaired arm must have been throbbing, because you didn't recover all that quickly from losing an arm. He had lost a bit of horsehair in the process, and he would take some time to get over that. That was Miss White's fault. She should not have grabbed him like that. You did not grab a Chinese poet. It was a very rude thing to do, and hot chocolate and barley sugar was not really enough to make up for something like that.

Richard's mother, Heather, was waiting for them on the lawn at the end of her driveway. She had binoculars strung around her neck; she would have been watching for their car as it climbed up the estate road. She always looked so calm, Virginia thought; so fresh, and on top of things. And she was always ready with one of her compliments, which she always seemed to mean. She said, as she greeted them when they emerged from the car, "You are a real marvel! Here you are, right as rain, after a really terrible shock. You're an example to us all! And you have such a lovely car. My car is black, but yours is that delightful blue. There should be more blue cars – we'd be a lot happier if there were."

Virginia laughed. "Does it matter? Cars should get you from one place to another – that's all."

Heather waved a careless hand. "Possibly, possibly. But look at Bella! Such beautiful hair! Wouldn't we give a couple of years of our lives just to have hair like that? I would. And look at her pretty dollies! Or are they boys? I believe they're boys after all." She smiled. "Boys don't like to be called pretty, do they?"

Bella looked away. She had never been sure what to say to Richard's mother and so had never said anything other than to agree with her. So now she said, "No."

Heather beamed. "Richard is so excited to be seeing you. You can go and knock on his door, and he'll show you his new trunk, all ready for the voyage. With his initials painted on it!" And to Virginia, she said, "I get terribly sea-sick, you know, but only for a day or two. Then it passes, and I emerge from my cabin. Fresh air is the only solution, you know, but they don't like you to open the portholes in case the weather gets up and everything is soaked. Did you hear about one of the steerage passengers last year who opened his porthole although he was right down below and the waves came in and he almost sank the whole ship?"

"You can imagine what the captain had to say," said Virginia.

"Oh, you certainly can, although captains are always very tactful. I think it's their training. They have to converse with all manner of people on board. It's a great art that some of them have. Others just drink, I'm told." She paused. "I'm staying at home for four months after I settle Richard. I'll spend some time with the girls. Then I'm coming back. Poor Jimmy is going to be on his own for rather a long time, but there we are."

"We'll have him round."

"You're a darling. Thank you. He loves company, and his bridge is improving – it really is." She looked away. "I'd prefer him not to spend too much time at the club. You know how it is. The bachelors and people. And that woman on the social committee, the one who looks like a paraffin refrigerator – she's shameless in the way she flirts with any spare man around the place – anything in trousers is fair game. She doesn't mean anything by it, of course, and that confuses the men. You know how they are."

Virginia nodded. "I suppose we should be sympathetic. Her husband has a tin leg."

"Yes, of course he does – poor man. It squeaks, you know. He should really oil it more frequently, but of course nobody can say that to his face. I'm surprised she doesn't do something about it. If my husband started squeaking I'd be there with my can of oil like a shot – like a shot."

In Richard's room, Bella was shown the trunk by its proud owner.

"Brand new," he said, stroking the domed lid. "It's made of wood and leather. The wood is really tough, you know. And you see that RM on the side? That's me – RM stands for Richard Macmillan."

"You're very lucky."

"I know." He paused. "You'll get a trunk too, when they send you to school. I suppose you'll go to one of those schools they have for girls. Some of them aren't bad, I think."

Bella shrugged. "I hope it's all right."

"I'm going really late," said Richard. "Most people are sent when they're seven or eight. I'm ten now. I'll only have two years – just – at this school until I go on to the next one, a pukka school."

She looked at him. It must be wonderful to be a boy – in spite of everything. Boys could do so many things. And yet they were so rough, and they fought, and their fingernails had grime under them – a black line. She glanced at Richard's hands. The black line was there under one of his thumbnails and under the nail of both index fingers. It was enough to make you shiver, although you shouldn't shiver when you were visiting people, if you could possibly avoid it. And there was something about Richard that was not disgusting at all – there was something that she really rather liked. He had a nice face. You might even have called him pretty, except that boys did not like that – his mother had just said something to that effect. But he *was* pretty – because of his nose, which was just the right shape, and that dimple he had, which was really unfair because boys couldn't care very much about dimples. It was girls who liked them, and yet they did not always get them. Dimples were wasted on boys.

He showed her a picture postcard. "This is the ship we're going to be on. See how big it is. They have deck games you can play. You know those rubber things you throw . . ."

"Deck quoits."

"Yes, those. And a fancy-dress competition. I've got a pirate's outfit – with an eyepatch. My mother's going to go as the Virgin Mary."

"That's a really good idea."

"Yes." He pointed to Li Po and Po Chü-i, who were tucked under her arm. "Why have you brought those dolls?"

She froze. "What dolls?"

He pointed again. "Those."

She affected surprise. "Oh, I'd forgotten about them. They're just a couple of old dolls."

He seemed unconvinced. "My mother says you say they can talk."

Bella forced a laugh. "Talk? Of course not. Why would I say that dolls can talk?"

He shrugged. "I don't know. That's what she said." He seemed to lose interest. "What about Miss White?"

"What about her?"

"Is she still teaching you?"

Bella said that she was. "I'd prefer to go to school."

Richard looked thoughtful. "If she went away, they'd have to send you to school. They couldn't let you get off lessons forever."

"That's true."

He made his suggestion. "You could ask them to fire her."

She frowned. "I couldn't."

"If she did something wrong, you could. You could tell on her, and they'd have to fire her. If she stole something, for instance. There's a man who works in my dad's office who stole some money. They fired him."

Bella was staring at his trunk. Imagine having your own trunk and setting off on a ship to England. Imagine that. Then she thought: Miss White may not have done anything wrong *yet*, but she would certainly like to – if she had the chance. She would like to get rid of her mother so that she could marry her father. What could be more wrong than that? And surely, if somebody was planning to do something wrong, then you were entitled to do your best to stop them before they had the chance to do it. It would be like putting out a fire before it took hold and burned your whole house down – it would be just like that.

She turned to Richard. "You know how people don't like other people to take away the person they're married to? You know about that?"

Richard looked smug. "I know all about that. I know everything about those things. More than you, I think."

She knew that she was on shaky ground. There was a lot that she did not know, and it might be best to get Richard to explain it – without revealing her ignorance, of course.

"You tell me what you know," she said. "Then I'll tell you if it's the same thing that I know."

He hesitated. Then, lowering his voice, he said, "Men and women make babies together, you know. They do that in their bedroom. At night time."

She shrugged. "Everyone knows that."

"Well, that's it," he said. "They take off their clothes. And then the baby starts."

This was new territory, but she did not want to show too much surprise. "Of course they do."

"But you're only meant to take off your clothes with somebody you're married to. Those are the rules."

She nodded. "That's right."

"So," he continued, "that's why men get really angry if other men take off their clothes with their wives. And the same goes for women too. If they think another woman has taken off her clothes with their husband, they get really cross."

She nodded. "That's the way it works," she said. "And you know something? I think Miss White is planning to take off her clothes with my daddy."

"I wouldn't be surprised," said Richard. "You should tell your mummy about that."

"Maybe I should."

Richard thought of something. "But you'll need proof. And you won't see her do that. She'll be far too cunning." He paused. "I've got an idea. What if you found some of your father's clothes in her bedroom? What if you showed these to your mother? Then she'd know, and she'd be able to fire her before it was too late and there was another baby. What about that?"

She weighed it up. She almost asked Li Po, who was good on this sort of thing, but stopped herself in time. "It could work," she said. "And it wouldn't be lying, because I know what she's planning."

Richard lowered his voice again. "Yes, you could find some of his clothes," he said. "You could say you found them under her bed. That's what you could do."

She blushed. Why not? He kept his clothes in drawers in his bedroom. Nikku ironed them and put them there. They would be easy to obtain.

Richard felt that the subject had now been dealt with. "Would you like to play Snakes and Ladders?" he asked.

She said that she would.

7

At the Club, in the Dining Room

Three days later, Virginia sent a message to Heather suggesting that they meet for lunch at the club. "I know that you're off in a week or so, and I can imagine how busy you'll be, but this is rather important. We need to talk." The message was delivered by Michael, on the ancient BSA motorbike he used to shop for provisions.

Heather gave Michael a reply to take back. "Dearest," she wrote, "of course I can meet you for lunch. Willingly. Actually, it will give me the chance to get out of the house for a little while. Every time I finish a task, there seems to be another that's crying out to be performed before I go. But the more I have to do, the longer it seems to take me to do anything. So, lunch with you will be perfect! I do hope that the important matter you refer to is nothing too serious, but even if it is, you will have my full attention and anything I can do to help – and I do mean anything – I shall do. *Voilà!*" Several words in this were underlined to add emphasis. Including *voilà*.

Virginia was not surprised by the tone of the response. Had she been in Heather's position, struggling to make domestic arrangements before a long sea voyage and months away from home, she would have found it difficult to be enthusiastic about lunch in the club. But then she was not Heather, with her unfailingly positive personality, with her underlining. *I am just me*, she thought: a depressing enough thought for all but the most incorrigible optimist.

She arrived at the club before Heather did and decided to go straight into the dining room to wait for her friend there. People often met for a drink on the veranda before their meal, and she noticed that there was already a small group of wives congregating there. A couple of them waved to her, expecting her to join them, but she declined, gesturing to indicate that she was expected inside. There was a copy of the *Ceylon Daily News* in the hall, and she picked that up and took it with her to her table. She started to read it, but she found that she could not concentrate. There was a disgruntled letter on the letters page, but she could not quite work out what the issue was. "Words cannot express my disappointment," the correspondent concluded. She sighed. *Words cannot express my disappointment . . .*

Heather arrived in a waft of freshly applied perfume. "I am ready," she announced as she sat down, "for the largest glass of sherry the club can provide."

"Don't ask for that," Virginia advised. "They'll take you at your word." She looked at her friend, who seemed unflustered.

Heather leaned forward. "I saw the paraffin refrigerator on the veranda – surrounded by her allies. They're planning something – I'm sure of it. A coup perhaps?"

"The committee can look after itself," said Virginia. "And they're welcome to it, anyway. Who in their right mind would want to run the club?"

Heather shrugged. "People want power, however small an amount is up for grabs." She paused. "But the real question is: *how are you?* Your note . . ." She left the sentence unfinished. The waiter had brought the menu, a small typed sheet revealing that the soup was pea and the main course was a choice between vegetable curry or toad-in-the-hole. There was ice cream for dessert – *flavours on application*.

They ordered. Then Heather resumed her questioning. "You don't have to tell me," she said. "The usual thing?"

Virginia looked down at the starched linen tablecloth, at the heavy EPNS cutlery with the club's initials etched into the handles, at the solid, predictable sameness of it all.

"Henry?" Heather persisted.

Virginia nodded.

"And your Miss White?"

There was a silence. Then Virginia nodded.

"I see. Where shall we start?"

The pea soup appeared. It was heavy and lumpy. "Do we have to eat this?" asked Heather. And then she answered her own question, "I suppose duty calls."

Heather laid aside her spoon after a few mouthfuls. "I just can't," she said. "I shall wait for the vegetable curry." She gave Virginia a look of sympathy. "It's just so obvious," she continued. "It's the reason, I suspect, why many people just won't consider taking somebody on to help with the children's education. This is what happens. There's no doubt . . ."

Virginia stopped her. "I'm not sure if it has actually happened. I can't be sure. At the moment, it's no more than a suspicion."

Heather looked doubtful. "When things get to the stage where one suspects, it often *has* happened. *The horse has bolted*, so to speak, although the stable door may be closed." The look became more sympathetic. "At least, that's what I've observed. This is hardly an unusual problem, you know. Any number of wives could tell you exactly the same story.

It's so . . . so *banal*, I think is the word. Yes, banal. So utterly expected."

"Something happened," said Virginia. "Bella made a comment some time ago. She said something about Miss White looking out of the window at Henry. She seemed to pick up something in the way she looked at him. I forget her precise words, but they left me feeling . . . well, a bit concerned."

"Children notice more than we give them credit for," said Heather. "We think they don't see what's going on, but they often do. They often know exactly what's what."

"I don't think Bella really knows about these things," said Virginia. "I mean, I don't think she knows the facts of life, or anything like that. She's only eight."

"Of course not," said Heather. "I don't believe we should burden children with these things before they're ready. I've discussed it with Jimmy, and he's pretty much of the same view. He says he'll have a word with Richard when he's thirteen, but he doesn't want him bothered by anything before then. Plenty of time, I always say." She paused. "But that's not to say that they don't know about *emotions*. They're different, aren't they? They may not know anything about the nuts and bolts, so to speak, but they can have a pretty good idea about whether people get on with one another. I suppose they probably have an inkling about love."

"They do," agreed Virginia. "They definitely do."

"So she picked up Miss White's interest in Henry. I see."

"I think she did. I may have misunderstood her, but I felt that. Then something else cropped up – something much more – how shall I put it? – concerning."

Heather was silent.

"Bella came to me a couple of days ago and said that

she had been in Miss White's bungalow and had found something."

"Been in it?" asked Heather. "Invited or uninvited?"

"Oh, she's always in and out of it. Miss White sometimes gives her lessons there – on the veranda."

"I see."

"She told me that she was there when Miss White had gone up to town for something or other. She said she went to get a book that she thought Miss White had left in her bedroom. So she went in and . . ."

"Oh now. They were there? Together?"

Virginia shook her head. "No, nothing like that. But . . ." She hesitated. Her embarrassment was clear. She spoke now with distaste. "She found an item of Henry's clothing."

Heather gave a start. "In her bedroom?"

Virginia nodded. "I'm afraid so."

Heather raised an eyebrow. "Oh dear. That doesn't look too good."

"Underwear," said Virginia, staring at the tablecloth.

She had not expected Heather's reaction, which was a peal of laughter. Concern became incredulity. "*Underwear?*" she exclaimed.

Her voice carried. At the other end of the room, a table of two couples paused with their soup spoons mid-air. Heather clapped a hand over her mouth, like a schoolgirl realising she had said something inappropriate in the presence of adults.

Virginia blushed red with embarrassment.

"It's all right," whispered Heather. "They didn't hear the context. We could have been talking about . . ." She waved a hand in the air. "About underwear in general. They are, after all, garments on which people have views."

Heather became serious. "I can't imagine there is anything

but an innocent explanation for their being there. People who get up to mischief tend not to leave their underwear in other people's bedrooms." She paused. "You see, if he had been . . . well, carrying on with her, and he then had to get dressed to go back to the house, would he have forgotten to put on his underwear? Surely not. Men just don't do that. They put their underwear on, and *then* they get into their trousers. Always, I'd say. Always."

Virginia sighed. "I know. That's what I thought."

Heather shook her head. "Very puzzling."

"Yes. But what am I to think?"

The waiter brought the vegetable curry. "Not too hot, Darmarathna?"

The waiter grinned. "Hardly any spices. Just a tiny, tiny bit." He held two fingers apart, almost touching, to signify a minute quantity.

He withdrew, and Heather continued, "I think there must be another explanation altogether."

Virginia waited.

Heather spoke slowly, weighing each word. "I'd suggest that Bella is making things up. I don't think she found the underwear there at all."

She looked at Virginia, gauging the effect of her charge. People were sensitive about their children, and she had just accused Bella of behaving in a way that, in an adult, would amount to criminal conduct. Of course, children were different, and were not to be judged for their misdeeds, but Heather feared Virginia might still take offence: a lioness will defend her cub, no matter how meretricious the cub may be.

Virginia was undisturbed. "But why would she do that?"

That was a relief to Heather. "Because she knows you're going to be shocked."

"Well, I was." Her reply was matter-of-fact.

"There you are – she knew exactly what the result would be. *Voilà!*"

Virginia wondered why Bella would want to shock her. Heather thought that was a question that might never be answered. Jealousy? Sheer bravado? Boredom? Hostility to Miss White because she made her work too hard? Misunderstandings over mathematics or French verbs? "You can take your pick. They get ideas in their heads, and off they go. They never think things through."

For a few moments Virginia pondered this in silence. Heather was probably right – the whole thing was absurd, and yet it was precisely the sort of scheme a child of Bella's age might cook up. But even if this were true, and Bella had conceived of some sort of ridiculous scheme to compromise Miss White, there were still the conflicting stories of what had happened in the Pavilion in the Clouds.

She had hardly made an inroad on her vegetable curry. Now she put down her fork. "There's something else," she said.

Heather dabbed at her lips with her table napkin before taking a sip of water. "Yes?"

Virginia told her about Henry's claim that the carpenter had spoken of rotten wood.

"I can see that happening," said Heather. "In this climate – with all this rain."

"But he didn't," said Virginia. "He was adamant. I spoke to the man himself, and he said there was nothing wrong with the wood."

Heather frowned. "Why would Henry deceive you?"

The question hung in the air – aimed at the heart of a marriage.

Virginia struggled. Henry had never lied to her before – as far as she knew. He was, by nature, a truthful man, and yet, on beginning an affair, the most truthful of men stray into deception. It was so common – and so easy. "Perhaps he wanted to hide something," said Virginia.

Heather looked puzzled. "I'm sorry, I don't quite understand. Hide what?"

"A failure on his part. He did say something about feeling guilty about my accident having taken place. He implied that he should have noticed a problem. Perhaps he just wanted to find a cause that would relieve him of at least some of the blame."

"The idea being that rotten wood would be difficult to spot? And, because of that, nothing to do with any fault on his part? Is that what you're saying?"

Virginia nodded. "Perhaps . . . Although I'm not really sure what I'm saying. I don't know what to think." She met her friend's gaze. "Don't you have times like that? Times when you just aren't sure whether you're quite getting what's going on?"

Heather stretched out and put her hand gently on Virginia's forearm. "Darling, I understand. Of course I do. You're trying to find an explanation that keeps everything intact – especially your marriage."

Virginia could not conceal her misery. That was exactly what she was trying to do. That was why she had contacted Heather – she wanted somebody else to say to her that everything was all right. She did not want to reach the unpalatable conclusion that she had been dreading. Above all else, she wanted reassurance.

Heather, who had been leaning forward, now sat up straight: she was resolved. "I think you need to act. You could spend a lot of time – and lose a lot of sleep – thinking about all this – trying to read things into this and that, trying to work out what – if anything – is going on behind your back. That's going to get you precisely nowhere." She paused, looking shrewdly at Virginia to see if she was carrying her with her. She decided that she was. Virginia wanted her to tell her what to do. That was why people asked other people to lunch at short notice. For some reason, this had happened to her many times before, in the invitations of various friends. Perhaps that's what I'm cut out to be, she thought: a shoulder on which others liked to cry. Well, there were far worse roles in this life.

"I'm not sure," Heather continued, "that your fall has anything to do with what may or may not be going on in the background. It may all be no more than a misunderstanding. But this extraordinary business of Bella and the . . ." she looked away with distaste, "and the underwear is a bit different. That may be a childish prank – I rather think it is – but there may be something much more serious underneath. She may have a feeling about this Lavender White – she is called Lavender, isn't she? Anyway, she may have picked up something very real, and that may be why she's trying to provoke an issue between you and her. Do you think that's possible?"

Virginia nodded. "Yes, I do."

"In that case, nip it in the bud. Get rid of her."

The waiter returned to take their plates away. Seeing the unfinished curry on Heather's plate, he enquired whether it had been too hot.

"No, perfect," Heather replied. "As ever. Now, what about ice cream? What flavours today?"

"No flavour, Mam."

"No flavour?"

"That means it is not vanilla or strawberry. It is something else. Nothing has been added."

"Perfect," said Heather, glancing at Virginia for

confirmation. "I think we'll both have that."

He retreated, and Heather quickly became business-like. "Terminate her contract – or whatever you call it. Pay her off. Problem solved."

"But we promised her at least another ten months." Where would Miss White go? Back to Calcutta, back to the circles she talked about, to the people who were almost the Governor of Bengal but not quite?

Heather made a gesture of resignation. "All right, but what's more important to you – ten months' salary in lieu of notice, or your marriage?"

"If you put it that way . . ."

"I do," said Heather.

Virginia looked doubtful. "What do I tell Henry?"

"You could tell him that you think she's coming between the two of you."

"I could say that," agreed Virginia. "Because it's true. She is."

But Heather had a warning. "The danger with saying that, of course, is that it could provoke a crisis. If he *is* having an affair, the hard thing for him might be bringing it out into the open. But in making the accusation, you will have done that for him. So it may prompt him to make a choice – and that choice, I'm sorry to say, might be her. You never know. *Men are tricky*. It's the way they're made."

"But . . ."

Whatever objection was forthcoming was brushed aside. "No, I'd be inclined not to say anything about that – rather, blame yourself. Say that you just can't get on with her. Say that you feel uncomfortable having her about the place. Say that she gives you the creeps. I've only met her a couple of times myself, but frankly I find her a bit creepy."

"I feel a bit sorry for her sometimes, I suppose." That was

true, and for a few moments she thought – with charity – of Miss White with her stories about Calcutta and St Andrews, and with the rouge she applied rather too generously to her cheeks, and with there being no question of any man in the background.

Heather understood her friend's reservations. "Fair enough, but you can't take the risk of anything developing, even if there's nothing at the moment. There's something odd going on, isn't there? Don't let it go any further. You have to take the plunge. Just do it. Make a bit of a fuss, but don't let on that you think he's been up to no good. That way you can let things get back to normal, and he'll probably forget all about it. Men do."

The ice cream arrived, and Heather dug into it with the long-handled spoon accompanying it.

"No flavour," she said.

8

The Music Goes Round and Round

Virginia decided to speak to Henry the following evening. They were together on the veranda as dusk fell, each nursing the drink that was their nightly sundowner – a gin and tonic for her and a whisky and soda for him. It was the best time of the day, she thought: Henry, tired from work, would be ready to relax, while she liked to watch the vestiges of day drain from the sky as the stars, as if on cue, made their appearance. It was also their time on their own, as Bella usually spent the half hour before her bath and bedtime attending to her scrapbooks. She had a shelf of these – bulging volumes into which she pasted pictures clipped from magazines and old newspapers. The scrapbooks were composed of rough grey paper; the glue she used she made herself out of flour and water. It took time to set, but it worked, and it did not have the smell of the glue that came in bottles. Li Po and Po Chü-i had scrapbooks too, that she maintained for them, although their taste in pictures differed from hers. Li Po liked photographs of food, while Po Chü-i liked pictures of birds. "You like very different things, don't you?" she said to them.

"We went to different schools," Li Po replied. "That is

why we are so different. One day I'll tell you all about those days."

Miss White was in her bungalow, from the windows of which squares of yellow light spilled out onto the lawn. She was playing her gramophone, and faint notes drifted through the semi-darkness – a tune she favoured, as they had heard it often enough.

"The BBC Dance Orchestra," said Henry, taking a sip of his whisky. "Listen to them. There they go."

It was 'The Music Goes Round and Around'. The lyrics, half heard, were distant, tinny things. *I push the first valve down, The music goes down and around, And it comes out here* . . . Virginia had once seen Miss White dancing to it on the veranda of her bungalow, dancing alone, until she realised that she was being watched and had stopped in embarrassment.

"Henry Hall," said Virginia. Her hand was shaking.

"He sings that other one, doesn't he?" asked Henry. "The one that Bella likes so much."

"'Teddy Bears' Picnic'."

Henry smiled. "I listened to the words the other day when Bella played it. A rather odd little song."

Virginia picked up her glass. It was cold to the touch. She took a deep breath. "Henry, I need to talk to you about Miss White." She spoke softly, keeping her voice down, although there was no chance of the governess hearing them across the two hundred yards of lawn that separated her bungalow from theirs.

She hardly dared watch for his reaction. She glanced from the corner of her eye and then looked away. He had not flinched. He had simply taken another sip of his whisky.

"What about her?"

"I want her to go."

He put down his glass. He frowned. Then he turned to her. "Why?"

The sky was almost dark now. A small flock of birds moved against the last streaks of light and was gone. A constellation, faint, just visible, dipped and swung above them, tiny points of white, pinpricks.

She kept her voice level. She was going to be firm; she was not going to become emotional. "I think it's time for her to go."

He picked up his glass and considered this for a few moments. Then he said, "But why? We told her she'd have another year."

"Ten months actually." It had sounded so little when she had first thought of it; now it was another matter.

"A year – ten months. Doesn't make much difference. Why now?"

She looked at him directly, trying to give the appearance of being surprised. "You don't want her to go?"

That might have been the challenge that she had wanted to avoid making – the words had somehow slipped out. And into a pool of silence, it seemed, as he was impassive – so much so that she had to glance at him to see whether he had heard her.

He had, and now he replied, "I don't mind either way. But it does seem a little harsh to show her the door when we told her that she'd be here until Bella went to school."

She was ready for that, as she had thought about it. "Bella could go off to school early. When Penny agreed, she said she could come any time." Penny was Henry's sister – the aunt in Edinburgh with whom Bella was to board. "She said that – remember? And I doubt if the school minds too much when she starts."

Henry lowered his glass to the table.

She said, "Have another whisky."

He looked at her quizzically. "You think I need it?"

Some of the tension drained away – but not all. She saw that he hesitated before reaching for the bottle. Was he worried about what he might say after another dram? That he might reveal what he really felt?

"I don't think you need it, no. But I know this may be a bit of a bombshell for you."

He poured the whisky into his glass and added a splash of soda water from the siphon. The carbon dioxide hissed. He turned to her as he lifted the glass. "Why?" he asked. "Why should it be a bombshell?"

"It's a change in our arrangements."

He considered this. "Arrangements change all the time." He paused. Then, "What have you got against her? I thought you took the view that she was doing a very good job with Bella. Look at her reading. And her French. She's got beyond that *plume de ma tante* stuff already. I even heard her say something in French to those dolls of hers. Heaven knows what it was, but she said it."

"Oh, I know. She's a very good teacher. I'm not disputing that."

Over the lawn, the music stopped, and then started again. The BBC Dance Orchestra remained on duty.

"If she's a good teacher, and Bella is happy with her, then couldn't you just put up with your . . ." He searched for the right words. ". . . with your feelings of irritation? I fully accept that she might keep us on our toes . . . *intellectually*." It was not a tea-planter's word, and he used it tentatively. "But she does the job, and we have to think of her perfectly reasonable expectations."

Virginia felt a momentary resentment. The criticism,

the distancing, the implication in the word he had chosen to use expressed an attitude she did not like at all. Henry and his friends may be suspicious of things of the mind, but she was not. That was the whole point of her reading circle: they were using their minds; they were asking questions. She was the intellectual equal of Miss White, even if, unlike the governess, she had had no university education. That had been because her parents had believed that her destiny was marriage and that higher education would be a distraction from that. And her mother had explicitly warned her that there were many men – possibly the majority – who were wary of a woman who might overshadow them in matters of the mind. "They don't like it," she said, "if you know more than they do. It's just the way men are. They like to be the leaders."

She had seethed at the unfairness of this and had tried to argue against what she saw as a self-defeatist view, but her mother simply smiled. "You'll find out soon enough that what I say is true," she said. "You'll see."

Miss White, it seemed, had understood this sensitivity and had been careful not to make much direct mention of her educational advantage. Although she pointedly referred to her father's academic standing, she only occasionally added that she, too, had been at university. "I was at St Andrews," she said. "Just like my father. My father teaches there, as I think I may have mentioned." Out of politeness more than anything else, Virginia had asked her what she had studied and had listened with a glazed expression as she listed the subjects she had included in her arts degree. "We all had to do the course in moral philosophy," she said. "Or almost all of us. It was regarded as an important cornerstone. Hume, you know." She paused. "David Hume, that is, the great Scottish philosopher. We had to read Hume."

"Of course," said Virginia, adding, "Hume. Of course."

Miss White looked at her as if trying to decide whether or not she had ever heard of him. "Sympathy," she said at last. "I always thought that people like Hume and Adam Smith were absolutely right when they said that sympathy lay at the heart of any moral system."

Virginia looked out of the window, towards the Pavilion in the Clouds, on the far side of the lawn. Two monkeys were playing on the structure's roof; one, having stolen something belonging to the other, appeared to be taunting its friend. A piece of fruit, perhaps. A nut from one of the trees.

"Do you think there's any sympathy in nature?" Virginia asked. "In monkeys, for instance?"

Miss White looked surprised. "Hume was thinking of human beings." It hardly needed to be said, she thought, but one should never underestimate the extent to which people could misunderstand things or would simply not take a common enough reference. She had met somebody in Calcutta who was under the impression that Camembert was a French revolutionary; or, rather, she had not actually *met* that person, but they had talked about him at a dinner party, and she had been as amused by this as everyone else, except, perhaps, the host, who had looked slightly anxious before he joined in the laughter. Camembert, of course, was not to be confused with Roquefort – now *there* was a convincing Jacobin.

Virginia was saying something. "Of course he was. I was just wondering, though, whether monkeys might not have the same . . . well, the same feelings as we do. I was just wondering." And she thought: *Do they know anything about monkeys in St Andrews?*

But Henry was looking at her, and she stopped thinking about Miss White and David Hume and that peculiar conversation they had had about monkeys. Now she turned to Henry, who was asking her, "Did you hear what I said to you?"

She shook her head. "Sorry. I was thinking about something else."

He was patient. "I was saying that I thought it might be a bit unfair to ask her to leave at this stage. She hasn't put a foot wrong, as far as I can see."

Virginia reached for her glass. There was still a small amount of gin and tonic in it, and she did not want to pour herself another one. She wanted to keep a clear head for this conversation. If she had another gin, then she knew what might happen. She might say what she really thought; she might come out and make precisely the accusation that she was resolved not to make.

"Oh," she said airily, "she's been all right, I suppose."

He looked at her with incredulity. "Just all right? Is that all? I think she's been far more than that. She's put in a real effort with Bella. She's spent hours – hours – reading to her. She's taught her all that Wordsworth. I've heard her. Wordsworth – and Bella's only eight. Can you point to any of the other children round here who know their Wordsworth?"

He took a further sip of whisky before he answered his own question. "I can't. Bella is streets ahead of any of the other children on any of the estates. Any. And the children from Colombo too."

"I'm not sure whether being able to recite screeds of Wordsworth is all that useful," she said quietly. "Children are more than little gramophone records."

"I never called them that. And Bella has learned plenty of other things. Her maths, for instance . . . She's run rings round young Richard, and he's said to be quite good at the subject. Jimmy told me he gets his tables a bit mixed up –

Bella never does that. Maybe there's a point to Wordsworth."

She stared at him. "But what about me?"

He frowned. "You? Wordsworth?"

Her irritation surfaced in her voice. "Not Wordsworth – I'm not talking about Wordsworth. I'm talking about the fact that I read to her too. I read to her a great deal."

He was placatory. "I don't deny that. I didn't mean to imply that you don't."

"I've taught her about the Chinese poets. She can recite some of the Wiley poems. You've heard her. She even named those dolls of hers after two of the poets. That was so sweet."

He became even more conciliatory. "My darling, I know all that. I know you've put a lot of effort into her education. And I'm proud of you – I really am."

That was probably true, she thought. He was proud of her reading circle; she had once heard him saying to somebody at the club, "My wife doesn't just play tennis, you know. She has a reading group. They read fearfully impressive books – you've no idea." She wished that her mother could have heard that – her mother, with her cutting remarks about how intelligence in a woman put most men off.

Now he reached across and touched her wrist gently, in a gesture of reassurance and appreciation. "Yes, I'm proud of what you do with your time."

Suddenly, she wanted to cry. She had looked about the landscape of their marriage, and she had discovered a rift, like a scar, a geological fault in otherwise stable terrain. There was something very wrong here – she was sure of it. There was something in his tone of voice – and in what he said – that was insincere. That was the way it sounded to her, even if she could not put her finger on the reason why this should be so. He was praising Miss White because at heart he wanted her to stay – and he wanted her to stay because the governess meant something to him. It may well be that he was not actually having an affair with her, but there was interest there. There was the potential for something more – and, whether or not he recognised that himself, it was still there, beneath the surface, waiting for its moment. That was what happened between men and women: there would be feeling under the surface, perhaps only dimly experienced; there were sentiments unexpressed, and then suddenly, without warning, there was the bursting of a dam within, and all restraint would be swept away. That happened – of course it happened. It had happened between her and Henry, after all. There had been nothing much on their first couple of meetings, and then, rather to her surprise, there had been a heady onrush of passion. It was as if they had both suddenly become intoxicated. They had both been surprised, in fact – Henry as much as she.

She looked at him. He was nothing special to look at. He might be described as presentable – just – but that would only be to a charitable eye. In a roomful of men you would hardly notice him – he would just be another man, the same as all the others, who would begin to put on weight and start to look battered by life, in the way in which men did. That was because they had to work all the time, just as Henry did, going off every morning to the office and tea factory. When he got up in the morning and looked out of their bedroom window, over the tops of the trees, over the morning mist, what did he have to think about but the long list of things he had to do that day? Whereas she had only to think about whether she might spend a further hour in bed before getting up for breakfast, and then have to decide whether she would have grapefruit or orange juice for breakfast, or kedgeree, or the spicy scrambled eggs that Michael liked to make for her. And then the day lay ahead quite empty, with

The Illustrated London News and Somerset Maugham and letters to write about the not very much that was happening. That was all. That was her life. But he was at the heart of it – this man whom she had married – whom she loved, she supposed, or was at least strongly attached to – what was the difference? You loved your old slippers; you loved your favourite bath salts; you loved your little daughter with her dolls and her dancing and her collection of butterflies, pinned to cardboard; you loved all those things, and you loved the husband who was part of all that. And if anything threatened that, then why should you not just make sure that it was simply not there to threaten it?

And then it occurred to her that if she ever had to do anything desperate to protect her world, she would do it – and have no compunction about it. She would fight to preserve what she had. She would do anything – *anything*. Unbidden, the troubling question arose: would she be justified in going so far as to push that woman off the Pavilion in the Clouds? She would, she thought.

Except, she had not done that. She did not bear that stain. But could Miss White do it? What if one looked at it from her perspective? What if she wanted to fight for something that was equally important to her? Would she show any compunction in doing the inconceivable? Or would she think: David Hume would never approve?

Henry said, "Darling, you're very dreamy this evening. I know this is an awkward subject, but we have to discuss it. It's a major decision."

She looked at him. "I don't want to discuss it, Henry," she said. "I've told you what I want. I just ask you to respect my feelings here. I'd prefer not to have Miss

White with us. That's all." She paused. "And I don't think I'm being unreasonable. I spoke to Heather about it, and she agrees . . ." She trailed off. She had not intended to mention her lunch at the club.

But it was too late. He had looked up with interest. "Heather? What's it got to do with her?"

She tried to make light of it. "Oh, we had lunch in the club the other day. I told you."

"You said you were going to play bridge."

She had forgotten that. Had she told him that? There was no reason, of course, why she should not have lunch in the club with Heather – wives met there all the time – but she had obviously not wanted him to know.

He became silent. She watched him. His silence, she thought, spoke volumes. She had been right in her suspicions.

"Very well," he said. "How much notice should we give her?"

She said the first thing that came into her mind. "Two weeks?"

He clearly had not expected that. He raised an eyebrow. "That's rather short. She'll have arrangements to make. Heaven knows what the poor woman is going to do. Do you have any idea? Do you have any idea where she might go?"

"We pay her fare," she said. "To wherever that's to be."

He sighed. "That's the least we can do – in the circumstances." Then he added, "And give her salary for the rest of the period we agreed before . . ." He hesitated, and then looked at her accusingly, ". . . before we changed our mind."

She said nothing, but nodded her assent.

He said, "Are you going to tell Bella?"

"Yes."

"She won't take it well, I fear."

But Virginia thought, *Don't be so sure about that – perhaps she will be getting exactly what she wanted.* She said, though, "Maybe. Who knows with children?"

9

Unpurified Water

Bella was looking at her scrapbook when Virginia came into her room. Li Po and Po Chü-i were sitting on two tiny chairs, doll's furniture, their arms hanging down on either side, their faces turned up to the ceiling. Li Po was asleep, she thought, but Po Chü-i was just thinking, as he often liked to do. He had a lot to think about, he had once told her: far too much to think about in the space of a whole day.

Virginia sat on the end of the bed and peered over Bella's shoulder at the open page of the scrapbook. There were several pages of pictures of royalty, for the most part cut from the pages of *The Illustrated London News*, a faithful observer of the doings of kings and queens. Here was the Duke of Windsor in Paris, walking in a garden with Wallis Simpson. "She has large pearls," Virginia said. "Look at her. Pearls, you see." And then, on the same page, was a picture from *The Times of India* of a maharajah bedecked with even larger pearls than the Duchess.

"They have fabulous jewels, those maharajahs," said Virginia. "Look at him – isn't he splendid?"

"Daddy doesn't wear jewels," said Bella, without looking up.

"That's different. Scotsmen and Englishmen don't wear jewellery. They just don't."

"But maharajahs can?"

"Yes, they can. It's the way they show the world how rich they are." She told her of a maharajah who had so many jewels that he had employed a courtier to walk behind him, wearing his excess jewels for him. "Fancy that! What a funny job for anybody to have."

It did not seem like that to Bella. To be the official wearer of a maharajah's jewels seemed like an enviable job.

Virginia looked up at the ceiling. "There's something we need to talk about," she began. "Something important."

Bella remained immersed in her scrapbook. She had turned a page now and was gazing at a picture of a whale breaching. Underneath this image, there was a pod of dolphins and a separate diagram of how a crab's claws worked. She traced the illustration of the mechanism with a finger.

"They could bite your finger off," she said. "A big crab could do that, couldn't it?"

Virginia glanced at the picture. "They could indeed. You have to be careful of crabs. And lobsters too. They have even stronger claws." She paused. "You know that you have to go home to school sooner or later. You're remembering that, aren't you?" It was like saying, Virginia thought, that you should remember that the world will end.

"Like Richard?"

Virginia seized on this. "Yes, just like Richard. He's going very soon now, isn't he? In a week or two's time, I think."

"He has a new trunk. It has his initials on."

Virginia said she had heard all about it. "He's looking forward to it, isn't he? He told you that, I imagine – when we went round to his house."

This brought a nod.

"So, you'll be going to school, just like Richard – except that you'll stay with your aunt Penny and your cousin. That'll be nicer than being a boarder, don't you think?"

"Maybe." She rather liked the idea of being a boarder. She had read stories about what boarders did: they had midnight feasts, they solved mysteries, they had best friends to whom they swore undying allegiance.

Virginia decided it was time. "We think – that is, Daddy and I think – that you'll go a bit earlier than planned. Quite soon, in fact."

Bella turned round. She fixed her mother with an intense gaze. "Next week?"

Virginia laughed. "Oh no, darling, not next week. We have to make arrangements. You can't just get up and leave, just like that. No, perhaps in a month's time. Or six weeks. It depends on the boats home. And also, we'll have to arrange for you to travel with somebody. There's bound to be somebody going."

Bella absorbed this information. She did not seem to be perturbed.

"And that means," Virginia continued, "that Miss White will be leaving. Very soon, in fact. Before you go."

"She has a big trunk in her bungalow. I've seen it. She can use that for her things."

She had expected more of a reaction. Children were at heart opposed to change; she had seen this so many times. They constantly surprise us with their bone-deep conservatism. They wanted the familiar, but they were also accepting.

"You'll be sorry to see her go, I think." Virginia was not sure whether she meant this as a question or an observation.

"Yes." But the scrapbook had reclaimed her attention. Now she was looking at a page of maps. There was a map of Ceylon. Underneath was printed, in large type, *The Pearl of the Orient*. Virginia read the inscription from where she was sitting. She had cut the map out for her from a brochure published by one of the tea brokers. We reduced the world to metaphor. A whole country was a pearl. For somebody to take away. To steal.

She stood up. This had been so much less difficult than she had imagined. That was because children were unpredictable. They accepted so much because they were used to things happening to them, rather than making things happen themselves. And then suddenly, at some point in their lives, the realisation dawned that the world need not be just something that happened to you, and that you could make it happen yourself. And you tried to do that, and you discovered that it did not always work.

"Miss White has been a very good teacher," Virginia said. "You've learned so much from her."

"Lots."

"Good."

There was silence. In the corridor, just beyond the door, Nikku was sweeping the floor, his broom bumping against the skirting boards. *I wish he wouldn't do that*, thought Virginia. *It chips the paint.* She sighed. Life could so quickly degenerate into an endless nagging of people to do this, to do that – to do things differently from the way in which they had always done them. So quickly could one end up complaining about everything because it failed to live up to standards that you felt you had to impose. They had no right to order these people about – she, at least, understood that, even if none of the others, none of the planters or their wives, understood that. We are *uninvited guests,* just as we are uninvited guests in every corner of the globe; and yet we take it upon ourselves to dictate how things should be done. That was the massive, almost unbelievable, conceit upon which the whole colonial enterprise was built, and yet which nobody seemed to see. She did not want to be here. She decided that she did not want this life she had created for herself, far away from everything, in a place that was alien however much you built your bungalows or planted your gardens. The jungle was just outside – thick, present, immutable. It did not belong to you. Nothing really belonged to you. You thought you could make it yours, but you were wrong. And now she was facing this entirely unnatural separation from her child, her only child. Oh, they talked about long trips home and how you could end up seeing a lot of the child in spite of everything, but that simply was not true. You gave up the child; you said goodbyes that could be for years, not months. And all the time those women who picked the tea, those women whose names she would never know because nobody bothered about them, those women at least had their children to go home to in the evening after they had put down those great baskets they carried. She closed her eyes. You could not think too much about these things, because there was a limit to the amount of pain you could stand without looking at the world through your tears, all day, every day.

"I've told her," she said to Henry. "I told her ten minutes ago. We had a little chat in her room."

It was mid-morning, on a Saturday, a day on which he only briefly called in on the tea factory. Now he was at home, on the veranda, eating a slice of toast and anchovy paste and glancing through a six-week-old copy of *The Scotsman*. He would read the newspaper carefully, fold it back into its original wrapper and then give it to Mr Maguire, his

Glaswegian assistant in the office. Mr Maguire would then read it himself before passing it on to one of his drinking companions in the club, a taciturn Aberdonian who was the up-country agent of a Colombo firm of hauliers. The Aberdonian had a local wife, who claimed to be a member of a Burgher family. She followed the Scottish news with fascination, revelling in the details of a distant and completely alien existence, as strange to her as any existence led on the shores of Greenland.

"And?" said Henry, licking anchovy paste from a finger.

"She took it very calmly. There was no reaction, in fact."

Henry was surprised. "I thought she might make a bit of a fuss." He sounded disappointed; he had warned Virginia that Bella could be upset, and he was not prepared for this. So he asked, "Are you sure?"

Virginia was certain. "Cool as a cucumber," she said. "She even said something about Miss White having a trunk in which she could pack all her things. She didn't express even the slightest concern. Nothing."

"That doesn't mean that she isn't feeling something," said Henry, stubbornly.

Virginia shook her head. "I think I can tell when something's worrying our daughter – and there was no sign of anything of that sort."

She watched her husband. His manner was restrained; it was as if he were calibrating his response to some standard of indifference. This was the dismissal of an employee they were talking about – not the banishing of a lover – and she imagined that he wanted to act accordingly.

Now Virginia made her suggestion. "I think you should have a word with Miss White now," she said. "You should tell her about our decision before Bella says something. We wouldn't want her to learn about it from her."

The effect of this was immediate. He stared at her in incomprehension.

"We have to speak to her," Virginia said.

He spoke falteringly. "Yes, but I thought that you would do that. Woman to woman, so to speak."

She held his gaze. She saw that his eyes moved away. "But you pay her," she said. "You're in charge of all the staff. You always have been."

"That's different," he said quickly. "She's not domestic staff, for heaven's sake. She's a governess." He laughed nervously. "I don't imagine she'd be pleased to be lumped in with the maids or the gardeners or what-have-you."

For a few moments she was silent. Then she said, "I'll speak to her. I'll go and have a word with her right now."

His relief was palpable. "Remember to reassure her about our honouring the contract." He looked at her anxiously. "Stress that she'll get full salary for the next ten months irrespective. And her fare, of course. The equivalent of a full fare home."

She nodded, and went off towards Miss White's bungalow. She could see the governess sitting on her veranda, reading a book. *Butter wouldn't melt . . .* she muttered under her breath, but then checked herself. She should not allow herself to harbour bitter feelings against Miss White, who was, after all, an old maid in the making. What must it be like to have no prospect of a husband, to know that one is plain, to know that men are simply not going to be interested and that one is going to have to spend one's entire life by oneself, as an adjunct to the lives of others? Poor woman; she did not deserve hostility even if she was desperate enough to seek to traduce another woman's husband under her very nose. *Under her very nose . . .* the words were sufficient to evoke renewed antipathy, and so she put them out of her mind, took a deep breath, and crossed the lawn towards the veranda from which Miss White was now watching her progress, the book lowered, time suspended.

It was easier than Virginia had imagined it would be – at least at the beginning. She went straight to the point, explaining that it had been necessary for them to change their plans at short notice. "Family factors," she said, adding, "quite unforeseen." And that, she thought, was true: it was indeed unforeseen that a rather plain, bluestocking-ish governess should set her hat at somebody else's husband.

Miss White nodded. "I understand," she said. "You'll be sending Bella off to school earlier than expected."

Virginia was taken aback. "As it happens," she said. "Yes, that's what we're planning to do."

"So you won't need me?" There was no resentment in the governess's tone, and now she went on to say, "There is always a terminus in this profession. Children grow up – sometimes rather quicker than we think they will."

"A *terminus*," muttered Virginia, as if savouring the unfamiliar word. Why could one not simply say an *end*? *Terminus* sounded rather like a bus-stop. "Yes, I suppose there will be a terminus. And I suppose we must be grateful that children grow up, much as we like them the way they are." She was grateful to Miss White for making it so easy.

"Well," Miss White continued, "I suppose it will be easier for her if she goes a few weeks early. That will mean she can settle in with her aunt before the school term begins. That would be better all round."

Virginia swallowed. "Actually, we were thinking of sending her much earlier than that. We thought that . . ."

Miss White's eyes had widened, and Virginia shifted uneasily under her gaze.

"Yes?"

Virginia struggled. "We thought that she might go next month – as long as we can get the passages booked."

"Next month?" Miss White exclaimed. She frowned, as if she found it hard to comprehend what had been said. "You mean in a few weeks' time?"

Virginia tried to keep her composure. "Yes. More or less. I mean, yes, I suppose."

Miss White lapsed into silence. Now she looked out towards the Pavilion, avoiding the glance that Virginia sent in her direction. Then she turned to Virginia and asked, "What about me?"

"Well, of course, Henry . . ."

She did not finish. "Am I to be sent home early too?" The tone of the question was icily polite.

Virginia tried to smile. "Heavens, no. Nobody's sending anybody home. But there's no point . . ." She made a helpless gesture. "There's no point in your occupying a position that's . . ." She searched for a tactful expression but there was none.

"That's ceased to exist?" offered Miss White.

"You could put it that way," said Virginia, weakly.

"I *do* put it that way. In fact, there are various ways in which you could put it, one of which is to use the term *to fire* . . . verb, transitive, meaning to dispose of the services of somebody."

"Oh, really," Virginia protested. "We certainly would not fire you."

"But isn't that what you're doing? If you're saying that there's no point in my being in my current position, doesn't that amount to a firing?"

Virginia's mouth was dry. A gin and tonic would have given her the courage she needed, she thought, but it was the wrong time of day. Even a glass of water would have helped.

She looked at Miss White. "Could you possibly give me a glass of water?"

Miss White was staring at her. It took her a few moments to answer. "Yes, I can get you a glass of water. I can certainly get you a glass of water."

"Fridge water?" Virginia asked.

Miss White was already standing up. She smiled, although the smile was far from warm. "Of course. Fridge water."

She went into the bungalow. Virginia sat back in her chair. She felt hot around the neck – she always felt that in moments of stress. The encounter had started off so easily, but that had been misleading. At that early point, Miss White was under the impression that her stay might be curtailed by a couple of weeks; her equanimity had disappeared very quickly when she discovered what was really entailed. The discomfort that she had expected before she came was now very real.

She waited. It was taking Miss White some time to fetch the glass of water. Virginia looked at her watch. It had stopped; she had forgotten to wind it, for the second time in three days. She looked at the shadows. There was a four o'clock feel to the day.

Miss White emerged holding a glass of water, which she passed to Virginia. "A warm day," she said. "I get thirsty in this weather."

She did not sound unfriendly. Virginia wondered whether the earlier frostiness – understandable, of course, in the circumstances – was simply a reflection of shock at the suddenness with which the information about Bella's impending departure had been conveyed. Momentous news might very quickly cease to seem momentous, once considered, even for a rather short time: for all she knew, it may even have occurred to Miss White that the situation had certain advantages for her. She had assumed that Miss White was content enough in her bungalow, with its views of distant hills and its cool breezes, but it was quite possible that she was bored. Who was there to talk to? She had that woman at the mission school whom she went off to see from time to time, and there were a few people at the club with whom she appeared to be on good terms – that man from one of the other big estates whose wife was always trying to organise talks at the club on obscure topics – most of them given by herself. They were friendly with Miss White, she had noticed, and there were one or two others – most of them on the periphery, and none in the social circles that really counted – she sometimes saw them with Miss White. But apart from that? She had made it clear enough that she regarded the ladies of the reading circle as being beneath her notice, and they had, understandably enough, reciprocated. That attitude of superiority had been shown in an early comment Miss White had made – a very hurtful one, Virginia thought – when she said, "Trollope, Trollope, Trollope – your reading circle certainly could not be accused of ignoring Mr Trollope." What was wrong with Trollope? And it was not true that they read too much Trollope. What about the Lawrence they had read, or the Sylvia Townsend Warner?

Virginia took hold of the glass. It was not cold; it was not fridge water. She hesitated. She looked at the water. She turned to Miss White and blurted out, "Your salary. Your salary's important."

She had intended to distract Miss White, and she did.

"Of course it's important," said the governess. "I work for my living."

"No, I mean it's important that your salary should be paid right up to the end of the original contractual period –

the period we agreed when you came to us in the first place."

As she spoke, Virginia lowered the glass of water to the floor beside her chair. She lifted her hand. Miss White was watching her. She saw Miss White's gaze drop, but the other woman was incapable of seeing what was happening on the floor.

Virginia blurted out, "And of course you'll get your fare home – or wherever it is you want to go."

Miss White said nothing.

"I'm keen," Virginia continued, "that is to say, *we're* keen – both Henry and I – that you should be as little inconvenienced as possible, and that you shouldn't lose anything through this change."

Miss White absorbed this. "Thank you," she said. It was a mechanical thank you – not one that sprang from real gratitude. *She's furious*, thought Virginia. And then she thought, *She hates me*, and after that she went on to think, *I shall not drink that water*. There was water that you drank – safe water – and water that you never drank, although the locals could survive it. She knew what it was like to suffer the stomach upset that went with drinking unclean tap water. In an extreme case you could even die. More likely, of course, would be days of pain as your stomach wrestled with the teeming malignant fauna that made their home in such water – the tiny organisms that could bring you to your knees, retching in agony. There was a man in the club who had been sick for months with a parasite he had ingested from an incautious draught of untreated water. She had seen him, standing by the tennis court, too emaciated and weak to play. "Water," he said, when she enquired after his health. And rolled his eyes. "I'll never make that mistake again."

Nor would she.

10

At the Club, on the Lawn

She had to see Heather, although her friend's departure for Colombo was now less than a week away. She sent a note with Michael, who rode up to the Macmillan bungalow and came back with the reply that although Heather would be unable to have lunch at the club, she was to be playing tennis there the following afternoon and they could have tea together afterwards. "I shall be ravenous," she wrote. "I always am after playing tennis, and we can get them to make us some sandwiches. Leave some room for sandwiches. 4 p.m. *Voilà!*"

When she arrived at the club, Heather was still playing a doubles match with three women whom Virginia knew, but not very well. They invited her to join them for tea, but Heather declined the invitation on her behalf. "We have to talk," she said, igniting their interest in gossip. One of the other players, wiping her brow with a small white towel, looked with interest at Virginia: a tête-à-tête in the club meant only one thing – matrimonial difficulties. There were so few opportunities for affairs in such a sparse population that when one arose how could others not take an interest?

They sat on the lawn, on wicker chairs under a large rain tree. A club servant, clad in a steward's jacket of starched white duck, brought the tray of tea and a jug of sweetened lime juice. The sandwiches to which Heather had referred arrived on a large plate, covered with thin muslin cloth to deter the flies. They were triangles of white bread, their fillings a mixture of cucumber and egg and cress. The bread was not yet stale but was on the cusp, curling slightly at the very edge, cut thin. "That, at least, is something," said Heather. "So many sandwiches are great lumps of bread."

"Is everything all right?" asked Heather, after her first sip of tea.

Virginia hesitated. Then, "No, not really. Well, perhaps." And finished with, "I'm not sure."

"Which means that it isn't," said Heather, putting down her teacup.

"No, probably not," agreed Virginia.

Heather shook her head ruefully. "I feared it would get messy."

"Did you?"

"Yes. Every time – every single time – these things start, they end up as a complete train crash. The only way out is radical surgery. Get rid of the troublemaker – see her off." She paused, and fixed Virginia with an almost accusing stare. "Did you do as I suggested?"

Virginia assured her that she had done so. "I spoke to Henry. I told him that I felt uncomfortable about having her in the house, so to speak."

"And how did he react?"

"He seemed to take it in his stride."

Heather frowned. "Guilt," she said. "He feels guilty. He can't show his displeasure because guilt is stopping him from doing that, and also, if he does, he'll be as good as confessing."

"I agree," said Virginia.

"And then?"

"We both took the view that she should get her salary for the full period of our original understanding. There was no argument about that."

"Fair enough."

"I suggested that he should tell her – that didn't go down at all well."

Heather managed a smile. "It wouldn't, would it? So you . . ."

"I said I'd do it. I went to see her. I didn't beat about the bush. I told her that we were sending Bella back earlier than we'd planned. She became quite distant. Cold, I'd say."

"Anger," said Heather, reaching for an egg and cress sandwich.

"I suppose so. And I'm not sure that I blame her. I'd probably feel the same if I were in her shoes."

"But you aren't in her shoes. And you have to remember that. You are a *wife*, Virginia. You are in the right here. This is your *husband* we're talking about. You have everything – and I mean *everything* – on your side. The law, the Governor, *God* even – if He has the time to take an interest in these petty matters . . ." She smiled at the thought. "After all, we ask God to do all sorts of things, don't we? To help us conduct our wars, defeat our enemies – even to win our tennis matches – which Molly and I didn't, by the way – my game was awful."

"It's because you've been so busy packing up. It must be so stressful."

"That's kind of you to say that. No, my game is just getting worse. I don't seem to see the ball coming. If the other side has a strong service, I'm done for. It whizzes past, and that's it."

Heather finished her sandwich and reached for another

one. "Where are things now? Has she accepted the *fait accompli*?"

Virginia looked away. She felt foolish, because what she was about to say seemed so improbable, when thought about here, in the open, on the lawn of the club, with the white-jacketed steward moving about on the periphery and the sweeper brushing away so energetically on the path that led to the flagpole. It was a scene that was implicitly endorsed by the law, the Governor, and, dared one presume, by God Himself. And yet the thoughts that had kept her awake the previous night were insidious and insistent, and she knew that she would have to share them with Heather if she were to regain her peace of mind.

"I spoke to her on her veranda," she began.

Heather nodded. "The best place for a conversation."

"Yes. We were sitting there, and I told her. But I was very thirsty for some reason – possibly because I was so anxious about the conversation we were due to have. Anyway, I asked her if she could give me a glass of water."

Heather waited.

"She went inside and then came back out with a glass."

Heather nibbled at her sandwich. "Yes?"

Virginia found herself lowering her voice. "You're probably going to think I'm being . . . what's the word? Imaginative? Over-nervous?"

Heather shrugged. "Highly strung?"

"No, not that. Suspicious . . . Yes, suspicious. You probably think I'm being too suspicious."

Heather held her gaze. It was exactly what she thought. But she said, "No, of course I don't." She hesitated. Virginia was a close friend – in so far as it was possible to have close friends in this lonely place, where everybody with whom one might develop a friendship was hours away. The winding

roads that led up the hillsides made every journey a long
one, not to say dangerous at times, when storms might wash
part of the road away. Tantalizingly, you might survey from
your veranda a bungalow across a valley, and know that
there were people sitting there looking right back – and yet
a painfully slow car journey lay between you and them. It
was a hard disease, this separation of friends. Virginia was
a friend, and you should not say to friends the opposite of
what one was thinking. And so now she said, "Actually, I do
– just a bit. I'm not suggesting that you have no grounds for
suspicion – I'm not saying that – but I think you may need to
control your imagination a bit. Just a bit . . ."

Virginia was quick to respond. "I thought you might
say that. And I don't blame you, I suppose. But anyway, I'm
going to tell you what happened and what I think about
it. Then, if you think I'm being ridiculous, please just tell
me. It's far better that way. Just say, *You're being stupid*. I'll
understand. No offence taken."

Heather reached for a cucumber sandwich. "I could eat
these things all day," she said.

Virginia declined the plate that Heather offered her. "I'm
not hungry," she said.

"Neither am I," said Heather, "but that won't stop me."
And with a quick *voilà*, she started to nibble at a small
triangular sandwich.

Between bites she said, "You were telling me about
Lavender White giving you . . ."

"Yes, a glass of water. I asked her, you see, for a glass of
water, and I reminded her that it should be from the fridge.
She has a fridge in her bungalow. The treated water is kept
there, just as in the main house."

"Of course."

"But the glass that she gave me was warm. It was

definitely not cold. It was *not* fridge water. That means she took it from the tap – the same source as bathwater, which is not treated."

Heather was halfway through her sandwich. She stopped eating. "From the tap? Are you sure?"

"Well, if it had been drinking water it would have been cold."

Heather finished her sandwich. She licked the tips of her fingers and then reached for her teacup. "We take it on trust that the club boils this water properly," she said. "You have to get it up to boiling point to make it safe."

"The club is good about these things," said Virginia. "They're meticulous. Mr Vandersan is very particular about hygiene." Mr Vandersan was the club administrator, the assistant to the secretary, a tall, imposing man, a member of a Burgher family. He invariably wore an aged panama with a green and red hat-band, symbol of some ancient club or school association. He was as firm with the staff as he was with the members, and any infringement of the club rules would be noted and solemnly raised with the guilty member. "There are always limits," he said. "The day we cease to recognise those limits is the day that everything comes crashing down."

Heather agreed. "The kitchens are spotless. I went in there once and was pretty impressed. And you're right about Mr Vandersan. He's wonderful." She remembered something. "You know the most extraordinary thing happened the other day – right here in the club. Joe Ellis was playing tennis with Bobby Phillips, and Bobby took his watch off and put it down beside the net – you know, on the ground near the post where you tighten the tension. He didn't want to damage it – apparently he broke a watch once with his powerful serve – actually broke the spring or whatever.

Anyway, he put the watch down, and they played a pretty strenuous set. Halfway through they nipped off to have a quick glass of lime juice. They were only away for a couple of minutes. They took up where they left off and in due course finished. Bobby went for his watch and . . . yes, no watch."

"Somebody had pinched it?"

Thefts in the club were rare. Mr Vandersan was careful in his choice of staff and would not tolerate any form of dishonesty.

"Yes," replied Heather. "Stolen. And of course who were the obvious suspects? The ball-boys. There were four of them – that cheeky little waif with the pointy head – you know him? – and his little pals. I rather like the fat one, but I haven't seen him recently. He was rather slow in running after the ball, but he had a lovely smile. His father cuts the grass – a nice man."

"Bobby asked the boys about it," Heather continued, "and there was a lot of head shaking. And then one of them said that there had been a man who had came onto the court saying that he was looking for a goat. I ask you: looking for a goat on a tennis court! Obviously this was complete invention, and Bobby was pretty sure that one of the boys had taken the watch. He called the groundsman over, and he searched the boys. Made them strip. No sign of the watch."

"Not much hope then," said Virginia. "They must have hidden it somewhere."

"Yes," agreed Heather. "But Bobby did not want to give up. It was a good watch, apparently, and had been given to him by his wife on their tenth anniversary. It had sentimental value."

"Understandably."

"So Bobby reported it to Mr Vandersan. He was livid. Bobby said he could almost see the smoke coming out of the top of his head, to which the panama hat served as a sort of chimney top. It must have been a real sight."

"Mr Vandersan said that he would deal with the matter and was confident he could get the watch back. Bobby was grateful but couldn't really see what could be done. The watch would have been spirited away, and the boys would probably wait a while before they tried to sell it. But you know what? Two days later he got a telephone call from Mr Vandersan to say that the watch was waiting for him in the club office and that he could collect it whenever it suited him. And do you know how he did that?"

Virginia shook her head. "No, no idea." She was impatient. She wanted to get back to the subject of Miss White: she was not interested in club gossip.

Heather laughed. "It's very funny, actually. Mr Vandersan told the boys that he knew a very powerful astrologer. He said that this man had mantras for all purposes – including one specially designed for putting an evil spell on boys. He said that if the watch did not find its way back to the club office, he would have a word with this astrologer and have a spell put on all four boys – innocent and guilty alike."

Virginia nodded. "The Tamils love their spells, don't they?"

"They do, and there's no better way of scaring the living daylights out of a Tamil than to tell him he's had a spell put on him. Their hair stands on end. They really believe it, and they'll rush off to get some mantra to ward off the evil eye. Those boys will have been quaking in their boots. Of course, the watch was found and returned."

Heather refilled their teacups. "Sorry. We need to get back to your glass of water. Did you drink it? Any ill effects?"

Virginia explained that she had discreetly left it untouched.

"Good," said Heather. "Of course, you can't be sure it was tap water, can you?"

Virginia looked puzzled. "But I told you: it was warm."

"What if the fridge wasn't working?" asked Heather. "Or if she had left the water jug out of it?" She gave Virginia a challenging look. "Possible, don't you think?"

Virginia had not thought of that, and now, as she did so, she felt a flush of embarrassment. It was such an obvious possibility that she felt ashamed to have failed to ask it. It was a demonstration, she decided, of just how excessively suspicious she had become.

"I hadn't thought of that," she said, lamely. "It's quite possible, I suppose, but I just wasn't thinking."

"On the other hand," said Heather, "she could have tried to poison you. I'm not saying it's impossible."

Virginia sighed. "I don't know what to think. I'm all over the place."

There was something in her tone that evoked Heather's sympathy. "Darling," she said, "you have every reason to feel a bit cut up over all this. You had a nasty, unexplained accident that might have been something to do with that woman – who knows?" She made a gesture of unknowing. "You've had to deal with a husband who *might* have a roving eye. You have no idea what's going on in your child's head – she *might* have seen something, you never know."

The litany of burdens was to grow longer. "And now you've got an aggrieved governess on your hands with whom you're going to have to put up over the next couple of weeks. None of that is simple – none of that is easy."

Virginia knew that; she wanted guidance, which Heather seemed unwilling to give. "So, what do I do?" she asked.

"Nothing," said Heather. "But you do nothing very carefully." She lifted her teacup, looking at Virginia over the rim. She had more to say, but she wanted to say it as gently as possible.

She started with an enquiry. "Are you sure about what Henry's thinking?"

Virginia looked puzzled. "About this? About Miss White?"

Heather lowered her teacup. "Not just that. About everything." She fixed Virginia with a penetrating gaze. "Sometimes we don't really understand men. We think we do, but we don't."

"You're talking about women? About wives?"

Heather nodded. "They're a different breed, you know." She smiled. "There are people who say that there's no difference between the way men and women think, but I can tell you there is. There's every difference in the world. You know that. I know that. Anybody who's ever lived with a man – anybody who's actually had a son – knows all about the differences."

Virginia hesitated. "Maybe . . ."

"No, definitely," Heather interjected. "The people who say that men and women look at things in the same way haven't got a clue – not a clue. It's wishful thinking on their part. Certainly, women who say that do so because . . ." She paused, looking for the right words. "Because they *want* that to be the case. Yes, that's it – they want to do the things that men do, and so they claim we all think the same way."

"You can see why . . ." Virginia began, only to be interrupted once again by Heather.

"Oh yes, you can see why they want that – and what woman wouldn't? What woman – whatever she may say to please her husband – doesn't want to be free to do the things that men do? To have the same chances in life?" She smiled. "I'm sounding a bit like a suffragette, don't you think?"

Virginia said that there was nothing wrong with that. "They had every reason to feel the way they did. And who would argue with them now?"

"Of course they did," agreed Heather. "Women are entitled to do the things that men do – of course they are. Men won't let us, of course, but we'll get there, I think. One day there'll be more women doctors and lawyers and others, and we won't have to sit here on lawns and drink tea and eat cucumber sandwiches."

"And egg and cress."

"Yes, and egg and cress."

They both laughed.

"But the point is," Heather continued, "that even if we claim what is owed to us, even if we stand up to men who belittle us, the fact remains that there's a big gulf between men and women in the way we think about things. There are plenty of things that men just don't see – they don't see them. And I suppose, to be fair, there are things that men see that we don't. A man can look at something and say, *Oh yes, such and such is going on*, and a woman can look at the same situation and see something completely different."

Virginia said that she thought that was probably right. She added that it had always been like that, and it would probably remain that way.

"The reason why I bring this up," Heather explained, "is that things can be going on in a husband's mind that his wife is simply unaware of."

Somewhere above their heads, in the overhanging boughs of a tree, a bird cackled in protest. They both looked up. Virginia said, "I love to hear the birds. That's one of the things I love about this country. The birds. And then I love the flowers and the greenery and the hills."

Heather glanced at her friend and then gazed up into the tree. "Yes," she said. "But you know that I want to be somewhere else. I want to go home, Virginia. I want to get back to where . . . to where you and I belong. We don't belong here, do we?" She paused. "You came here when you were tiny, I know that, but that doesn't mean that you belong here, does it? We've come here, we went to India, we went all over the place, and thought that we owned the place, but we don't really, do we? And when we go, we know what will happen. We know, don't we?"

She pointed towards the club house, to the tennis court, to the tea gardens that could be seen on the nearby hillside, neat lines of green. "All that, you see, all of that will go. And the jungle will come back and cover it all."

Virginia shook her head. She did not disagree with what Heather had said about not belonging, but she was not so sure about the jungle. "I don't think so. I think that there'll be people who'll just step into our shoes."

Heather looked surprised. "Do you really think so? Do you think there'll be people who can actually be bothered?"

"Yes. The Sinhalese are clever people. Some of them rather look down on us, you know. And you've got the Burghers too. Look at them."

"Oh well," said Heather. She picked at a sandwich. "Men, though. What about men? The reason why I raised the subject, I suppose, is to ask you whether you are *sure* of Henry. I don't mean to be nosy – I really don't. I just feel that you need to consider whether something might be going on that you haven't picked up on."

"An affair? That he's getting involved with that woman?"

Heather did not reply immediately. She lifted a corner

of the sandwich to examine the slices of cucumber within. "What I was wondering," she said, "was whether there was any possibility that Henry and Lavender White were acting . . . well, acting together. Acting to . . ." She held the sandwich in one hand; the other hand she waved in the air. "Whether they have something in mind?"

It took Virginia a few moments to realise what was being suggested. Then, "Plotting against me?"

"I didn't want to say that," said Heather. "But yes. And I'm sure the answer is no. I'm sure that Henry wouldn't . . ."

She left the sentence unfinished. She had spotted Mr Vandersan, who was walking purposefully across the lawn towards them. As he approached, he lifted his hat. "How nice to see you two ladies," he said. "Is everything satisfactory?"

Heather beamed at him. "It certainly is, Mr Vandersan. Lovely sandwiches."

Mr Vandersan beamed. "Cook is a wonder – even with sandwiches. We are very lucky to have him."

"You must hold on to him," said Virginia.

"Indeed we must, Mrs Ferguson. You'd be surprised at how many members try to poach him from us. Oh, my goodness me, I could tell you a story or two. Shameless attempts at enticement of an employee. It should be a criminal offence, in my opinion. Well, perhaps that's a bit extreme, but it's certainly bad behaviour. How would they like it if I came and pinched their tea pickers? Or their own cooks, for that matter?"

There were a few remarks about the tennis court and the cutting of the lawn, and then, lifting his hat a final time, he returned to the club house.

"A very fine man," said Heather. "I've always liked him." She glanced at her watch. "Time marches on, I'm afraid."

"I must let you get back."

Heather rose to her feet. "Perhaps I shouldn't have said what I said. I don't want to alarm you."

Virginia rose too. A small beetle had dropped down from the tree onto her skirt. She brushed it off in spite of its attempts to hang on to the material.

"I wouldn't think too much about all this," said Heather. "The situation is going to resolve itself soon enough. Two weeks is not a very long time."

They walked together to the car park. Mr Vandersan watched them from the window of his office. Spotting that they had noticed him, he raised a hand to wave, a gesture that seemed almost like a benediction.

Bill Was Weak

Miss White was scrupulously polite over the days that followed but was clearly upset at the prospect of leaving early. While she had been in the habit of having dinner in the main bungalow on four days of the week, eating alone in her own dining room on the other days, now she excused herself from those social occasions. She did this on the pretext of having a great deal to do. "I have much to arrange between now and then," she said to Virginia, emphasising the *then* as if it were some day of reckoning that was fast approaching. "I have an entire household to pack up, and much else to do besides. So, if you'll forgive me, I shall not be having dinner with you."

Virginia made a half-hearted attempt to persuade her to do otherwise, but both women knew that neither wanted to sit together at the same table.

"If there is anything I can do to help," said Virginia, "I'm at your disposal. You know that, of course."

Miss White inclined her head almost imperceptibly. "You're very kind, but I think that everything's under control."

It was a favourite expression of hers – *everything's under control* – and Virginia had always found it vaguely amusing.

She had a vision of things going haywire, and of Miss White trying to bring them back under control, running backwards and forwards in an increasingly desperate attempt to restore order.

"Henry can arrange with the agent down in Colombo to make bookings," Virginia offered. "Mr Pessoa is very good at these arrangements."

Mr Pessoa was a member of an old trading family, formerly spice dealers, who, when not attending to his business in Colombo, lived in a rambling merchant's house in the old fort at Galle. This house was run, it was said, by one of the last eunuchs from the defunct Ottoman court.

"I'm sure he is," said Miss White. "But I have already sent a telegram to my friend down there asking her to arrange my passage to Calcutta."

"You'll be looking forward to that. You're fond of Calcutta, aren't you?"

Miss White pursed her lips. "I hadn't anticipated being back there so soon," she said. "But, be that as it may, I shall enjoy seeing old friends."

Again, the emphasis was pointed: *friends*, as if it were reliable friends who were currently in short supply.

Virginia ploughed on regardless of the implicit rebuke. "Will you be looking for a governess's post? Presumably there will be many families only too keen to have you."

Miss White shook her head. "Education has its rewards, undoubtedly, but it also has . . ." She paused, and looked directly at Virginia before adding, "its disappointments."

Virginia pretended not to pick up the reproach. If anything, this exchange confirmed her view that she simply could not have Miss White about the place much longer. Calcutta could not beckon too early, she felt.

Bella's lessons continued during this period, although

Miss White seemed to make less effort. Mistakes in the work-books in which Bella did her mathematics or wrote her English essays were left only partly corrected: whereas in the past Miss White would have written out a misspelled word in red ink in the margin, now she simply put a small cross against the word and wrote *dic* beside it – an instruction to go to the dictionary and check the right spelling of the word in question. French was entirely abandoned, apart from the occasional *bonjour*, and mathematics suffered a grave reduction in the number of men set to their Sisyphean task of digging ditches.

Arrangements had now been made for Bella's trip. Heather would be taking Richard back to school and would be happy to have Bella accompany them. She would be going to Edinburgh anyway, on her way to settling Richard in, and it would be no trouble, she said, to hand Bella over to her aunt. Ideally, Virginia would have accompanied her on the voyage and seen her safely set up with Henry's sister, but Heather's offer would mean that she would not have to leave Henry alone for two or three months.

There were reasons why she did not want to do that. There were stories that circulated of what might happen during a wife's absence – stories of flings with other men's wives, conducted on trips to Kandy or Colombo – or of liaisons with local women that blew up spectacularly on the wife's return. In one case, the wife was said to have returned early and to have discovered the local woman actually living in the house, her clothes hung alongside her own outfits in the wardrobe. The shame of that must have been unbearable, thought Virginia: how could anyone recover from something like that? Of course, it might have been no more than one of those stories that are embroidered or even invented by people who had nothing better to do than to pass on idle gossip, but even if it was apocryphal, it was a warning to any wife who would spend too much time away from home.

No, this was not a time to leave Henry alone for several months, and so she gratefully agreed that Bella should travel with Heather and Richard. Packing began, along with the commissioning from the local tailor of new clothing for the voyage.

"You'll look very smart in your new outfits," said Virginia, and fought back a surge of emotion. This was her child she was sending off to the other side of the world – the child who had been at her side for all her eight years of life, the child she had kissed each night at bedtime, the child whose entire life had been lived under her care. She was sending her away because that is what you did, no matter how unnatural, how cruel it seemed. This wretched empire! Why did we have to have it, if it split people from family in this way? Other peoples did not have to do any of this. The Italians did not deprive themselves of their children in this way, nor did the Norwegians or the Austrians, or anybody, really: just the British, and the French and Portuguese, to a degree, because of their rambling, far-flung empires that were going to come to an end at some point, surely, because all empires in history did that – sooner or later.

She almost spoke to Henry about it but held herself back at the last moment. She wanted to say to him, "Couldn't we just sell up and go back to Scotland? Wouldn't it be somehow simpler?"

That was the problem. It would be far simpler not to hold on to far-flung possessions and cultivate one's own backyard for a change. You would not need a vast army for that; you would not need all this loneliness and separation and . . . what else was there? Fortitude. Suffering. She knew a little bit about Buddhism – one could hardly be unaware of it in Ceylon – and she knew that it counselled against the tyranny of possessions. If you had only those things that were required for your immediate needs, you would enjoy far greater freedom than those who had a great deal. And surely there was something to be said for not having to worry about what was happening in the tea factory or the amount of cash available to pay the workers, or to buy fuel for the generators that produced the electricity that dried the tea, that made the money for all of these things. Freedom from the bondage of material things – that surely was a goal worth pursuing, even if you ended up donning saffron and chanting.

But then there was hot water, and the comforts of clean sheets, and food served on bone-china plates, and trips to Colombo, and *The Illustrated London News* and the gramophone. If these were part of material tyranny, then it was a comfortable tyranny that one would have to be awfully high-minded to give up. And perfume, of course – one should not forget perfume and sandalwood soap sent out from London. Perhaps if Buddhism were more accepting of these things, then it would be easier to be a Buddhist.

She did not speak to Henry. One day she would do so – she would tackle him about what lay ahead of them, rather than conveniently pretending that the future would sort itself out. She would ask him to set a date, a terminus to their life in Ceylon, when they might go back and farm somewhere in the Borders, near Melrose, perhaps, and enjoy the company of neighbours and townspeople, and go shopping in Edinburgh, at Jenners, and not be lonely and cut off from all the latest things.

Henry was busy. The price of tea was abnormally high, and this was an inducement to increase production before the market corrected itself. It was a feature of tea production that fluctuations in the price could wipe out a whole month's profit during the time it took to get the finished product down to Colombo; Henry had seen this happen to people he had known, some of whom had been ruined within the space of a few weeks when a whole crop had been dried too quickly or too fiercely, or had been packed when too damp and had become mouldy. One of the planters had simply walked away after a series of misfortunes, and Henry had been able to understand why he had done it, even as others talked of cowardice and weakness of character. He had been unable to meet his wages and had been pressed by the bank in Colombo to pay off a mushrooming overdraft. People did not understand the pressures under which a small or marginal estate might work. To abandon everything like that was cowardly, Henry thought, but might people not be forgiven – occasionally – for being human?

It had been the talk of the club for weeks, if not months, and Henry had participated in some of the discussion.

"I knew Bill was weak," said one of the members in the bar. "But I had no idea just how weak he was."

"And Helen – poor woman – left behind to pick up the pieces," said another, of the planter's wife.

"How many wives are in that position, I wonder? Thousands."

"Mind you, some bring it upon themselves. There are some shrews . . . I'm not justifying it, of course, but they can drive a man to distraction."

"He was probably planning to leave her anyway. That's the sort of chap he must have been. Carrying on with somebody and all the while planning to skedaddle." That was Henry who said that.

"Despicable," muttered another member of the group.

Henry nodded. "Unfortunate," he said.

"There are bolters of both sexes," said the man who had started the discussion. "Both can come out of the stables if things get too difficult."

"It's not easy," said Henry, "to keep women entertained up here. What's there for them to do? Tennis? Bridge? My wife reads a lot. She runs out of books, actually. We at least have our work."

"For which nobody in particular thanks us," said another.

"Does anybody thank anybody?" asked Henry. "For anything? I only ask." He paused. "And what do we get out of it? We see our lives slipping away from us. We work all hours of creation. We have people coming to us with their problems all day, every day. We're dog-tired when we get home. Home leave is a long time off. And so it goes on and on."

They looked at him.

"No use complaining," said one, and the others nodded. What was wrong with Henry? If everybody started talking like that, they might as well pack up. You had to believe in what you were doing; if you started to question things, you were finished. Everybody knew that, even if very few people spelled it out. Was Henry weak, like Bill? Was he going to surprise them? Not Henry, surely, who had never faltered, as far as anybody knew, and whose estate was run on model lines. No, this was an unguarded thought of the sort that we all had from time to time, and that meant nothing very much. So his comment was ignored, and the conversation moved to other topics.

Henry had to be in Colombo overnight. He would make the journey to Kandy by car and then take the midday train to the capital. There was a dinner to mark the retirement of a government official who had been helpful to the tea estates – four or five of the planters would be attending, and they would travel together. "Not that I particularly want to go," he said to Virginia. "I have better things to do than sit through interminable speeches. You know what it's like." He gave her an enquiring look. "You'll be all right?"

"Of course I shall. I'm not going to be on my own. And Miss White . . ."

"Of course," he said. "She'll be in her bungalow. And I can get Michael to sleep in the kitchen, if you like. Just so that there's a man about the place."

"We'll be fine. Don't worry."

He nodded. "He snores anyway. You'd hear him throughout the house."

She smiled. "He has an awfully big nose, poor Michael. It's a bit like a trumpet. That would account for the snoring." She thought of the cook's wife, a small, timid woman who hid her face behind a headscarf when you looked in her direction. She had borne him five children and put up with years of snoring too. Poor woman.

"You sure you'll be all right?"

She was. "You go. Try to enjoy yourself."

Suddenly it occurred to her that he might not be going with the other planters; he might be going with Miss White. The unwelcome thought came as a shock, and her expression registered this. He noticed, and said, quite sharply, "What?"

She sought to cover up her surprise. "Nothing."

"You looked as if you'd thought of something."

She shook her head. "I hadn't. Just odd thoughts. Nothing to do with anything."

She watched him motor down the drive that linked the bungalow with the estate road. As he reached the junction, he sounded the car horn, wound down a window and waved.

The sound of the horn reminded her of the steam train's whistle. That wistful blast punctuated the trip from Kandy at intervals of a few minutes, whenever the train negotiated a corner or approached a bridge, or when it neared a station, in a cloud of hissing steam, and people were milling about on the line, seemingly indifferent to the approach of the engine. There were so many people – so many – and they kept coming; whenever anything happened, people would materialise out of nowhere and watch with dark, wide eyes. Henry slept through the noise, cocooned in the padded seat of his first-class compartment, unaware of the stares of others. He could sleep all the way from Kandy to Colombo, he said, which was the reason why he chose to travel by train rather than make the journey by car.

Bella was finishing off a lesson with Miss White then came to see her mother in the pavilion.

"Ask Michael to bring a tray of tea out here," Virginia said to her. "And lemonade for you. There's some cake, I think."

Bella had been carrying Li Po and Po Chü-i. She put the dolls down on a small table, arranging their limbs for comfort. "They like cake too," she said. "Po Chü-i in particular. He is much greedier than Li Po. He often has more than his fair share."

Virginia gave Po Chü-i a disapproving look. The doll looked back at her, shameless.

"Gluttony is one of the vices," she said sternly. "Does Po Chü-i know that?"

Bella replied that she doubted it. "He is not nearly as clever as Li Po," she said. "Li Po knows much more than his brother."

"Are they brothers, then?" asked Virginia.

Bella looked thoughtful. "Sort of brothers. Sometimes

they are – sometimes they are not. It all depends."

Virginia smiled. "That's interesting. I thought they were just friends."

"Oh, they are friends too. They're best friends. They're blood brothers, actually."

That interested Virginia. Her own brother had revealed to her once that he had a blood brother – his friend at school – and that they had sealed their bond with the mingling of blood from razor cuts on the palms of their hands. She had been horrified. "You could die," she warned. That was a good way to get blood poisoning – and if you got blood poisoning, then you died. Everybody knew that. But he had laughed, as one might laugh at some piece of pre-scientific superstition. "You don't understand. Blood brothers don't die from blood poisoning. It's not like that."

She had felt envious. She had never heard of blood sisters. Boys, it seemed, had so much more fun.

"He's my best friend ever," her brother continued. "If I ever had to save his life, I would do it. Straight away. No thinking. I'd save his life."

"And mine?" she asked. "Would you save my life too?"

"Possibly," he said. "But that's different."

Now she looked at Bella and said, "You could try to make Po Chü-i a better doll."

This brought a snap response, and a look of reproach. "He's a poet. He's not a doll."

"Of course."

"Po Chü-i gets really angry if he hears somebody calling him a doll. I have to tell him that they don't mean to be rude, but he still gets angry. He says that people should know better than that."

"Of course they should," said Virginia. "And I'm very sorry if I offended him."

"He says it's all right. He said he knows that you won't do it again."

Virginia nodded. "I still think you could tell him not to be so greedy. I'm sure he'll listen to you."

Bella went off to ask for the tea and lemonade. While she was away, Virginia reached into the large wicker basket that she kept beside her chair in the pavilion. This was where she put out-of-date magazines once they had been read – they were removed from the large magazine canterbury on the bungalow veranda to this basket. She found an old *National Geographic*. She liked the pictures; she enjoyed the prose, with its slight air of the cinema travelogue. There was an article on the North American woodpecker and one entitled 'Men and Gold'. Throughout history, the article said, men have been unable to resist the allure of this beguiling metal – it adorns and beautifies, just as it corrupts. She looked at the woodpeckers and began to read about them, but her mind soon wandered. She was thinking about Henry. She loved him; of course she loved him, and she was sure that he loved her. She had been imagining everything. It was inconceivable that he should have strayed. Why should he? She looked at the two dolls. They were impassive.

Bella came back, and the tea and lemonade followed her. They looked at woodpeckers together. "I don't like those birds," said Bella, wrinkling her nose in disgust. "They look horrid."

"They're all right," said Virginia.

Bella shuddered. "They could hurt you with those beaks. Look at them."

"Woodpeckers never attack humans," said Virginia.

Bella looked at her anxiously. "Are you sure?"

"Yes, absolutely sure." She smiled. "There are other

things to think about, darling. You needn't worry about woodpeckers."

They paged through the magazine. Virginia poured herself a cup of tea and sipped at it while Bella drank the homemade lemonade from her glass. It was too sweet for the adult palate, but children loved it. She thought of the letter she would write Penny in Edinburgh, asking her to watch the amount of sweet things in Bella's diet. And she would have to tell her about how some things gave her a mild rash if she ate too much of them – pumpkin, oddly enough, did that. There would have to be a list of requests – tactfully put, of course, because they were imposing on Penny's kindness. The alternative, of course, was for Virginia to go back, to leave Ceylon, and set up home in Scotland. Some wives did that, but it meant that they never saw their husbands more than once a year, and what was the point of being married if you were to spend most of your time apart? Those marriages rarely survived the prolonged separation. Women could cope with that sort of thing, but not men, because so many of them simply could not be by themselves for any length of time. Men were weak; they looked so strong, sometimes, but that was misleading. Men were weak.

Virginia looked at her watch. Time was an emptiness. It was a billowing, echoing void. We threw events into it, as we might throw stones over a cliff, or into a well, and lose sight of them. Nothing was anchored; nothing was permanent. She looked up at the sky and thought of how small our concerns seemed when viewed from somewhere up there, somewhere impossibly far away. We were just a little rock hurtling through space, and we were the tiniest things on that rock, for all our ambitions and anxieties. What did any of our human concerns matter from that perspective? *National Geographic* certainly understood that: the latest issue, still in the house, had an article that suggested the sun would burn out and explode in a few billion years, but before it did that it would burn our earth to a crisp. We would become cosmic dust, it said. If that was our fate – and the astronomers seemed agreed on it – then did it make much sense for us to treat our brief moment too seriously? She sighed. She would like to be able to discuss this with somebody, but who was there? Henry would not understand, or would simply say, "Be that as it may," which was what he said about anything beyond his immediate comprehension. Heather? She would quickly move the conversation back to a subject of her choice – she always did that. Miss White? The governess, even when they had been talking to one another, would have curled her lip and implied that she had already thought about these things and knew the answer but would not expect Virginia to be able to understand that.

She saw that it was now four o'clock and that there were three hours until dinner. She would have a lie-down, perhaps, and a brief nap. Then she could run a bath and luxuriate in that for half an hour before it would be time for a sundowner and perhaps a game of draughts with Bella. Miss White had taught her how to play, and Bella had become an adept at the game. There seemed to be a ruthless streak in her – a determination to win that she, Virginia, rarely felt. That was strange. People differed when it came to competitiveness. Heather, for instance, liked to win at tennis and could sulk if she lost, and there were one or two other women at the club who were the same. Virginia was indifferent to the result – and when she told Bella that it did not matter whether one won or lost, she, unlike many parents who gave the same message, actually believed it. So many of the things we told our children, she thought, we did not believe. She did not believe that there were three wise men from the east, nor that there was a primeval garden with an apple tree, nor that Noah built himself an ark and its precise length was three hundred cubits; she believed none of that, and yet she herself had solemnly told Bella about these things, reading to her from a book called *The Sunday-School Book*. And we had to believe in something, she told herself, because the truth sometimes seemed too thin to satisfy our yearnings.

She said to Bella, "I'm going to go inside and write a letter before I go for a little nap. Do you want to stay out here?"

Bella was undecided, but then she nodded. "For a little while."

"Keep away from the edge." It had been secured now, with a new barrier, but Virginia still felt wary.

Another nod.

"And then come back in in about ten or fifteen minutes. You might like to tidy your room, and then we can play draughts."

Bella grinned. "I'll beat you again. I bet I'll win."

"It doesn't matter whether you win or lose," Virginia began.

"It does," said Bella. "It does matter. You want to win."

Virginia smiled. "We'll see."

*

Virginia occupied herself with writing a letter to her parents. Her father had retired now, and, having left Colombo, they were living in a village outside Dumfries, in the south-west of Scotland. Their life, she suspected, was a small and constrained one – her father had an arthritic hip that prevented him getting about, and her mother occupied her time with the affairs of a rural women's institute. She had

written to them about their decision to send Bella back early
– now she had more details to give them, about the place she
was to get at George Watson's Ladies' College in Edinburgh,
about the arrangement with Penny, about how she herself
hoped to come home for a good long stay – four or five
months – in the summer of 1940, when Henry was due to
take his long leave.

"I try not to worry," she wrote. "We read what is
happening on the continent, and it makes me very anxious.
Henry says that we are unprepared because we haven't spent
enough on the armed forces. He says you have to make
sacrifices if you want to defend yourself properly. He says
that too many people have been looking the other way and
that doing that just won't work.

"I don't think the Germans will ever be satisfied. Hitler
will want more and more because he's promised so much to
his people. And they love it when he picks on defenceless
people – they cheer the bully on. There are some Jewish
people in Colombo who have been raising money for Jews in
Germany who have lost their homes and businesses to those
thugs. I feel so sorry for them because so many of them have
no other home and people don't seem to want them. Can you
imagine what it feels like to know that other people don't
want you? We've never felt that because we've always been
so fortunate, but sometimes I stop and think about it, and I
can hardly bear it."

She had begun to write about the birds she had seen in
the garden when she heard the scream. She let go of her pen,
and a drop of ink fell onto the page of the letter. The ink blot
spread quickly, sending out tiny rivulets through the fibres
of the paper. She stood up, her heart racing. Had that been
Bella?

She thought of the pavilion. She should not have allowed

her to be there by *herself* – what had she been thinking of? She let out a little cry – almost a sob – and pushed her chair back. She got to her feet, and stumbled. She picked herself up and ran from the room. She cried out, "Bella!"

From the veranda, as she rushed to negotiate the steps down to the lawn, she saw two figures in the pavilion, and her heart gave a leap. Bella had not fallen over the edge, and Miss White with her. Now she saw Miss White push Bella away and then bundle her out of the pavilion, half lifting her, half shoving her. Virginia ran down the steps and across the lawn. She almost tripped on a croquet hoop, but it was ripped out of the soil and clattered to one side.

Miss White was shouting, and Virginia realised that this was what she had heard in the bungalow – she had heard the governess rather than Bella. The relief overwhelmed her; she almost stopped where she was; she felt her legs become unsteady beneath her; she almost sank to her knees.

But now Miss White had noticed her and was shouting something that she could not quite make out. The governess shouted again, and this time she pointed towards the lawn in front of Virginia.

"There," Miss White shouted. "There. There."

Virginia stopped. She had seen something on the grass, and it was moving towards her. For a few seconds, she froze, but then she moved sharply to one side. The snake, an elegant slithering shape, shot past her, its long body moving from side to side as it made its escape. Its neck and head were slightly raised, and she could see from the half-extended hood that it was a cobra.

Now she ran across the rest of the lawn until she reached the pavilion. Bella was on one of the steps that led up from the lawn; Miss White stood behind her, her hands on the child's shoulders.

"A cobra," said Miss White. "There was a cobra."

Bella threw herself at her mother, hugging her. "Mummy . . ."

Virginia comforted her. She looked up at Miss White. "What happened?"

"I was on my veranda," Miss White said. "Thank heavens I came out. I saw Bella out here, and I saw that there was something on the floor in front of her. Then it moved, and I knew what it was. My heart stopped. It actually stopped. I ran across . . ." She paused. "I think it must have seen me, and it decided to shoot off. Thank God. That was it on the lawn in front of you back there."

"It's gone now," said Virginia.

She hugged Bella to her. The little girl was shaking. Virginia looked at Miss White. "I don't know what to say," she half whispered.

Miss White said, "No need to say anything. No need at all." Her tone was controlled, but Virginia noticed that her hands were shaking.

12

It Was a Big Snake

Virginia shepherded Bella back into the bungalow. Neither said anything until they were inside, when Bella, who had Li Po and Po Chü-i tucked under her arm, took one in each hand and addressed them gravely.

"You were very brave," she said.

Virginia smiled. "Of course they were. But you were brave too, darling. It's important not to frighten snakes. They go away if you don't panic them. You did the right thing, I think."

Bella nodded. "It was a big snake."

Virginia agreed. She shuddered. It was best not to think about what might have happened. It was a nerve poison, was it not, cobra venom? It attacked the nervous system and your breathing. She closed her eyes briefly. Then she said, "What happened? Where did it come from?"

They were now in Bella's bedroom, and she laid Li Po and Po Chü-i down on her bed. Turning to her mother, she said, "I knocked over your basket. You know the basket that you keep your magazines in? That one."

"And the snake was behind it?"

Bella shook her head. "No, not behind it. It was in it."

Virginia stared at her. "You mean . . . Inside? Inside the basket?"

"Yes. Inside. When the basket fell over, the lid came off. That's how the snake got out. He was very cross. He put up his neck thing . . ."

"His hood."

"Yes, his hood. Like that. You know how they do. Remember when we were in Colombo visiting Mr Pessoa? Remember? And that old man came to the gate with his basket, and he had that big snake. He played his pipe, and the snake danced. Daddy gave him money. He was a very smelly old man."

"He was." She thought quickly. "But the lid was on, you say? Are you sure?"

Bella did not hesitate. "Yes. You always keep the lid on that basket, don't you? It stops your magazines getting wet if it rains and some rain comes into the pavilion."

Virginia looked away. She needed to compose herself. She did not want to frighten Bella, who had been shocked enough as it was. "So the snake had been trapped inside the basket, and when you knocked it over it escaped? Is that what happened, darling?"

Bella was matter-of-fact. "Yes. That's what happened." She turned to Li Po. "You saw it, Li Po, didn't you? You saw the snake come out of the basket. You saw it."

Li Po agreed. "I saw it," he said.

"You see?" said Bella.

"See what?"

"Li Po says he saw it. He says the snake came out of the basket."

Virginia glanced at the doll. "I wonder if Li Po knows how the snake got into the basket," she said, trying to keep her tone even. "He often sees things we don't see, I suspect."

Bella liked this. Most of the time, adults failed to grasp things under their very noses, but occasionally they did – as with now. She looked directly at Li Po and asked him. Then she turned back to face her mother. "He says that somebody must have put it there."

For a few moments Virginia was silent, but then she said, "Why would he say that, do you think?"

Bella shrugged. "He didn't tell me why. But I think I know why."

"Which is?"

"Because snakes can't open lids. Even Po Chü-i knows that."

Virginia felt her heart beating within her. Delayed shock, she thought. It is sometimes only well after an event that you feel the impact, she had read somewhere. They called it delayed shock.

Bella had begun to tidy her dressing table. Her ribbons were in a muddle; now she began to disentangle them. She said to her mother, "Miss White saved me, I think. Otherwise, I'd be dead."

The words hung in the air.

"You mustn't talk like that," said Virginia. "It was a nasty moment, but the snake probably would not have bitten you. They don't like to bite, you know. They're just defending themselves."

As she said this, she remembered that she had fished in the basket for that copy of *National Geographic*. Had the lid been off it? She did not think so. She always replaced the lid. It had almost been blown away once, and since then she had made a point of ensuring that she replaced it. But then she thought: had the snake been in the basket when she put her hand in for the magazine? If so, there had been two narrow deliverances that day. But why was there a cobra there, anyway? Cobras did not like high altitudes; it was just too cool for them where they were. They were snakes of the lower plains and the coastal jungle. They liked the warmth.

She watched Bella sorting out her ribbons. At least she was none the worse for the experience. Children were like that: they could experience the most dreadful things, and they would bounce back as if nothing had happened, their resilience an effective emotional armour against all but the most devastating blows. She would do nothing to disturb that now.

"Would you like me to read you a story?" Virginia asked. "Perhaps you'd like some more lemonade and a story. On the veranda?"

Bella looked thoughtful. "Could we invite Miss White?"

Virginia hesitated, but only for a moment or two. "Of course. Would you like that?"

"Yes," said Bella. "She saved my life, you see."

"Darling, I'm not sure if that's absolutely true. She certainly helped, but I don't think we'd say she actually saved your life. That's maybe going a bit too far."

"No," Bella insisted. "She did. She saved my life."

Virginia swallowed. "Well, let's not argue about that. I'll go over and ask her. We've got some lemon drizzle cake, I think. She might like a slice of that."

They sat on the veranda. The sun was sinking low, a great red ball over the hills to the west, and the sky had that very distinctive pale wash of the day's end. A small flock of parrots, squawking in outrage, rose from a treetop, swooped and dipped, before descending on the branches of another tree.

"Silly birds," observed Miss White. "They're always making a fuss about something."

Virginia was trying her best to be cheerful. "I must admit I love them. I love green birds."

"I like the paradise fly-catcher," said Miss White. Turning to Bella, she asked, "And you, Bella? What's your favourite bird, do you think? Of all the birds you can see in the garden, which one is the nicest?"

"I like tiny birds," said Bella. "You know those little ones. They sit on the window sometimes."

"I know the ones you mean," said Virginia. "I forget what they're called. They're very pretty."

Suddenly Bella looked at Miss White. "I'm very sorry," she said.

Miss White looked puzzled. "Sorry about what? About the snake?"

"That wasn't your fault," said Virginia, sounding bemused. "You don't need to be sorry about what happened." Children, she knew, could blame themselves when things went wrong.

"No, not that," said Bella. She had fixed Miss White with an earnest stare now, and the governess looked uncomfortable, shifting in her seat and glancing at Virginia as if to solicit support.

"Oh well," said Miss White. "What an exciting day it's been – not that we'd want too many of these."

Bella persisted. "I want to say sorry."

Virginia reached for the teapot. "May I top up your cup?" she said to Miss White.

Before Miss White could answer, Bella continued, "I put some of Daddy's things in your room, Miss White. That was me. I'm really sorry."

Nobody moved. Virginia had been lifting up the teapot

to refresh her cup. She froze, with the teapot half inclined but not yet pouring. Miss White had been reaching for a piece of cake; she, too, was still, her hand poised above the cake-stand.

Virginia found her voice first. "Darling, you mustn't make things up." She laughed, as if to suggest that what had been said was absurd. "I have no idea what you're talking about."

It was the wrong tactic. Now with all the resentment of the wronged, Bella protested, "I'm not making anything up! You know what I'm talking about. You're the one who's fibbing."

Virginia put down the teapot. "I wish I did." Indulgence became disapproval, and her tone was now severe. "I think you should go to your room and think about your behaviour."

This was to pile outrage upon insult. "I'm not telling fibs," said Bella, her voice rising in indignation. "You know that I'm telling the truth. I put Daddy's things in Miss White's room so that you'd think she was going to steal him away from us. And you did. You thought that, and you're making her go – all because of me."

Miss White was pale. She turned her head slightly, away from Bella, so that she was now facing Virginia. "Really?" she said, her voice not much louder than a whisper.

"It's complete nonsense," snapped Virginia. And to Bella, "You mustn't let your imagination run away with you, darling."

Bella started to cry. "I'm not telling fibs," she sobbed. "I really did it. That's why I want to say sorry. Miss White saved my life, and I can't *not* say sorry."

Unexpectedly, Miss White reached out and put her hand on Bella's forearm in a calming gesture. "I believe you, Bella."

Virginia opened her mouth to say something, but no

words came. Miss White turned to look at her expectantly, awaiting a comment.

Virginia did not rise to the challenge. "I really don't think we should talk about this any further," she said.

Miss White frowned. After a few moments, her reply came in measured tones. "I'm inclined to agree. Damage done is damage done."

"But I want you to know I'm sorry," said Bella.

Miss White glanced at her but did not say anything. Bella waited. Then Virginia said, "I suggest you have your bath now, Bella."

Bella seemed to be waiting for a further word from Miss White, but none came. Now the governess pushed her chair back and stood up. "I shall be returning to my bungalow," she said.

Virginia rose to her feet. "I'm sorry about this misunderstanding," she said. The apology sounded lame and seemed barely to register with Miss White. Turning on her heels, the governess left the veranda with a brief word of thanks for the half-finished tea and cake. Virginia groaned.

"Look what you've done," she whispered to Bella.

Bella looked defiant. "You can't make her go. You have to change your mind."

Virginia shook her head. "We can't undo anything at this point," she said. "Miss White has made her plans. So have we."

"I want her to stay," said Bella.

"She can't. And you have to go off to school."

"I hate you," said Bella, picking up Li Po and Po Chü-i.

"Darling," said Virginia, stepping forward to embrace her. "Please don't be upset . . ."

But Bella escaped her embrace and ran back down the corridor to her room. Virginia looked about in despair. She had created this situation – it was her fault. Dishonesty came back to haunt one – she had been told that as a child and knew that it was true. And here was the proposition illustrating itself once again. She had deliberately chosen to get rid of Miss White for something that she had no evidence she had done, and this was the result: embarrassment and exposure, both richly deserved, both effectively impossible to do anything about.

Dinner for Virginia and Bella was a strained affair. They ate early, as Bella would need to get to bed, and they ate largely in silence. Virginia did her best to deal with the tension that had arisen and told Bella that as far as she was concerned, the unfortunate incident was over and done with. "All I would like you to remember," she said, as gently as she could, "is that we don't always say the things we're thinking. I know that you like to be truthful, but . . ."

Bella glowered at her. "You said I was making it up. You said that to Miss White."

Virginia remained composed. "Did I? Well, that was probably because I didn't want her to be hurt. People can be hurt by things that other people say. You know that, don't you?"

Bella looked down at her plate. "Yes," she muttered. "They can be hurt by fibs too."

"Of course they can."

"Or by being told to go away when they've done nothing wrong."

Virginia bit her lip. "There were reasons why it's best for Miss White to go a bit early. And the most important one is that you're going back home. You wouldn't want to change that, would you?"

"No, but it's still unfair that she's being told to go away."

Virginia shook her head. "Darling, nobody is being told to go away, as you put it. Daddy and I decided that it would be best for you to start school a bit earlier – that's all."

Bella folded her hands. "I was very unkind. I tried to turn you against Miss White. It was very unkind, and God is going to punish me for it."

"Nobody is going to punish you for anything," said Virginia. "Least of all God. He has far too many other things to worry about."

Bella was not reassured. "I feel very bad," she said. "I feel so bad I could be sick."

"You're imagining it. Eat your pudding. You like tapioca, don't you?"

Bella lowered her head. She had done what she could. But she still felt bad, and thought that she would feel bad for a long time. She stared at her plate of tapioca and then pushed it away from her.

Virginia said nothing. Children had their moods. These things passed. She was thinking of what, if anything, she needed to do. Perhaps she should be frank with Miss White. Perhaps she should tell her exactly why things had happened in the way they did. She should clear the air with an honest disclosure – then it would be up to the governess to decide whether she wanted to leave on good terms, or leave with a cloud hanging over all of them. She owed that to her, perhaps, especially after today, when she had undoubtedly saved Bella from at least a very high risk of being bitten by the cobra.

The cobra . . . A thought occurred to Virginia. Somebody had put the cobra there, and had done so to imperil her – she was the only one who used that basket. But who would be so perverse as to do something that could also harm somebody else – especially a child? It could be the same person, of course, who had interfered with the pavilion barrier. But who would have done that? Who would want her dead? Anybody?

Heather's warning at the club came back to her. But that was ridiculous. If Henry and Miss White were having an affair, then surely the simplest thing for them to do would be to run off together. Why would they want to get her out of the way and risk the consequences that would follow were they to be found out? It did not make sense.

Suddenly it came to her that there was a simple and certain way of finding out whether Henry was involved with Miss White. She would offer to go with Bella to settle her in Scotland, leaving Henry by himself. If he were having an affair with Miss White, that would suit him perfectly, and he would be enthusiastic about the suggestion. They would be free to enjoy one another's company for three or four months while she was away. It would be a perfect opportunity for them. She paused. On the other hand, if he thought, as was perfectly possible, that it would be best for Bella to have her mother accompany her – he might be willing to remain in Ceylon by himself not because of Miss White, but because he wanted what was best for Bella. She sighed. She had previously thought that her life on the estate was far too settled and had yearned for more excitement. Now she would have welcomed a return to simplicity. She wanted to get back to a time when nothing happened, and when this nothingness passed in a quiet and untroubled succession of uneventful days.

The generator up at the factory was switched off slightly early that night, as Virginia had been warned it would be. A small amount of maintenance work was required on it, the factory manager had told her, and would she mind if the power were to be shut off half an hour in advance? She had agreed but had forgotten about the arrangement until it happened, and she was plunged into darkness while still sitting at her desk, writing a letter. Bella was safely in bed, her light already out, Li Po and Po Chü-i on the pillow beside her. They knew, of course, about what was going on because they saw it all. And they knew, too, that theirs would be the last laugh – knowledge that sustained all the dolls, all the stuffed animals, all the familiars of the young. Bella lay there, staring at the ceiling, on which muted patterns of moonlight shone faintly through a chink in the curtains. She was thinking of Miss White and what she had done to her – a terrible thing, the enormity of which was far outweighed by her attempt at an apology.

"I didn't mean it," she whispered to Li Po. "I really didn't. I thought . . ." She could not find the words for what she had thought.

Li Po was impassive. Sometimes he was like that; he kept his own counsel and was tantalizingly silent, even when a few words would make things so much better.

"You believe me, don't you? You know that I didn't mean to hurt Miss White."

He could hardly ignore the directness of the plea.

"You could always tell Daddy," he said.

She had not expected this, and it took a few moments for her to respond. "But he'll be cross with me." She could not tell him; she simply could not. What would he think when she told him she had taken his clothes – stolen them, really. He had never raised a hand to her, never smacked her, even when she had done things that had shocked Li Po and Po Chü-i into silence, but perhaps this would be an occasion when the only punishment severe enough would be a hiding. Richard had told her that his father had given him a hiding when he had tied a firework to their dog's tail – and he had admitted that it was a terrible thing and he had not realised that the dog would be so upset by it. He had been sorry that he did it, because he loved their dog, and he had never been cruel to it before. "He ran away, wailing his head off, and hid under a bush, and they had to send the gardener's boy in on his hands and knees to drag him out. I felt so bad. I was really sorry. Poor dog. And then my dad gave me a hiding although I'd already promised that I would never do anything like that again."

The story had made a strong impression on her, and she remembered it now. There was a world of harsh justice that governed the affairs of boys and men; it did not seem to affect girls and women in quite the same way. Mind you, they didn't do the sort of things that would bring retribution down on their heads. Boys did things like that, of course, because boys were . . . well, boys were a bit stupid. But some of the things they did were not so stupid and were exciting, and made her think that all the time boys were having more fun and laughing at girls because they could do all those things that girls were not allowed to do. What use were boys anyway?

"If you decide to tell Daddy," said Li Po, "you could tell him when he comes home tomorrow."

She tried to make out his expression – to see whether he looked really serious when he gave this advice, but it was too dark, and she closed her eyes again. She was not very sleepy.

In the drawing room, where Virginia had her desk, she rose to her feet and found one of the oil lamps kept ready for use on a side-table. She pumped it up and put a match to the mantle. Then she lit another one, and the darkness was dispelled.

She walked over to the window that gave onto the veranda. In the distance, across the lawn, she saw a light appear in Miss White's bungalow. The curtains of her living room, which faced the main house, had not been drawn, and for a few moments she saw Miss White silhouetted by the light. And the sight somehow made her realise what she had to do.

She left one of the lamps where it was on the table and took the other one with her. She did not like going anywhere in the darkness, even with a lamp, but it would be a short walk across the lawn to the other bungalow. And if she kept her eyes on where she was putting her feet, she would see exactly where she was going, and there was no reason to imagine that the cobra would be anywhere near at this stage. They very rarely saw snakes, and cobras, she told herself, were such rare visitors anyway. It would be far away by now, heading down the hill, going back to wherever it had come from, to the warmth of the lower ground where cobras felt more comfortable.

She called out as she approached the dark mouth of Miss White's veranda. "Only me. Only me."

The thought occurred to her that she should be careful not to give the governess a fright by appearing unannounced at her door. She was, after all, armed, and although nothing had been seen of her pistol, it was still there, she assumed, and might be used. What if Miss White were to shoot her? People occasionally shot other people, and it was exactly in these circumstances that they did so. There had been that case down in Kandy where the young English wife of one of the civil servants had shot her husband in the course of an argument. The bullet had lodged in his leg and had not done much damage, but it had been the talk of Ceylon – or part of Ceylon – for some time. She had not been prosecuted, because the husband had backed up her claim that it was an accident, but the wife had confessed to a friend, after having too much to drink one evening, that she had actually been aiming at his toes because she had discovered that he had been having an affair, and it was only his sense of guilt that had made him back her story. It was a shocking business, but it was another example of how dangerous it was to have guns in the house.

But she put the thought out of her mind. Governesses did not shoot people. It was entirely unheard of. Miss White was harmless.

She called out again, "It's only me, Miss White. Me. Virginia."

There was silence, followed by the sound of footsteps, amplified by the movement of floorboards. Miss White's bungalow had creaky floors – Henry had promised to have them fixed but had never got round to it. He was too busy; there was just too much to do. "I can't do everything," he had said, peevishly. "People expect me to do this, that and the next thing, but there are limits." Now the floorboards protested loudly in the darkness as Miss White approached.

She stood in the doorway, holding a lamp. "I was about to go to bed," she said. Her tone was unfriendly.

"Please could we speak? Just for a few minutes."

"About?"

Virginia felt the back of her neck get warm. The governess must know what this was about. She was being disingenuous.

"About what was said earlier on. About what Bella said."

Miss White did not reply immediately. The lamp hissed as the fuel sprayed on the mantle. Then, eventually, she said, "I'm not sure that there's much to say about that. And I have decided to bring forward my departure to the day after tomorrow."

That was unexpected. Virginia gasped. "Oh, you mustn't. Please . . ."

Miss White stepped aside, indicating that Virginia should come into the bungalow. It was a grudging invitation, but Virginia said, "Thank you. I won't keep you long."

They went into Miss White's living room, where another lamp, throwing out a soft white light, stood on a small table in the middle of the room. Virginia sat down, and then Miss White did so too, choosing a chair facing her visitor. Neither woman relaxed.

"I feel very badly about this whole business," Virginia began. "And I thought I should just tell you how I feel. Perhaps I should have done this some time ago. I'm sorry."

Miss White stared at her. "Nobody is obliged to wear her heart on her sleeve," she said.

Virginia swallowed. The other woman was not going to make it easy. "I feel that there was a bit of a personality clash. I know you're very good at your job – nobody would doubt that for a moment – not for a moment. But at the same time, I felt . . ." This would be the difficult part. "I felt that it was inherently hard sharing my home, if you understand what I mean."

Miss White arched an eyebrow. "I believe there are two roofs here," she said icily.

"I know, I know. But we are very isolated, as I'm sure you'll agree. But sometimes one just wants to be by oneself – in a marriage, that is. You find it hard to share your home."

Miss White's expression was impassive. "I see. Well, that's your prerogative. It's your home. I'm just a . . ."

She did not finish. Virginia raised a hand. "Oh, please don't talk like that. We value you very highly."

Miss White spoke slowly. "What I wonder is this: where did Bella get those ideas about . . . about your husband and me? Where did that come from?"

Virginia hesitated. "I might have said something without thinking. She may have misunderstood me. Heaven knows."

"I see."

Only now did Miss White look away. "I know what you think of me," she said. "You think I'm one of those desperate spinsters who'll always be on the edge of things. Who'll never have a man of her own . . ."

"Oh no. No. I don't think that at all."

But Miss White seemed determined to continue. "People think that way, you know. They really do. But they'd be surprised. I have had . . ." She paused. "I've had many offers."

"I'm sure you have."

Miss White sniffed. "You're just saying that. You, like a lot of people, think I'm on the shelf."

"I don't." She did.

"I'm not, as it happens. I have had . . . well, I've had many lovers."

Virginia struggled not to laugh. Miss White . . . many lovers? This was ridiculous, but it was also slightly pathetic. Whoever boasted of having had many lovers with any degree of credibility? Certainly not rather plain governesses.

Miss White was staring at her. "You do know," she said, "that men find me attractive? You know that?"

Virginia's eyes widened. "Men find you attractive? Well, of course they will. I don't doubt that."

"I'm not sure if you really mean that."

Virginia said nothing. She did not see where the

conversation could go, and she now thought it a mistake to have gone over to Miss White's bungalow in the first place.

Miss White now got to her feet. She said, "I'm going to leave the day after tomorrow. I have friends in Kandy with whom I'll stay. I'll arrange for my things to be collected."

She moved towards the door, and Virginia knew that the conversation had come to an end. As she left the veranda, she turned and said to Miss White, "I hope you and I can continue to be friends."

Miss White moved back from the half-closed door. She had not heard what Virginia had said. "I'm sorry, I didn't hear you," she said.

"I said that I hope you and I can continue to be friends."

She took a step back into the darkness of the house but then came forward so that she was standing in the doorway once again. "Oh, were we ever friends? Do you think we were?" The question was posed without much expression – as if it were a dispassionate enquiry, about something of little significance.

Virginia was about to answer – to protest that she had always considered them to have been friends – but Miss White did not stay for an answer. The door was closed, not quite slammed, but shut decisively, and then there came the sound of a key turning in the lock. Virginia turned and began to walk back across the dark square of the lawn. The lamp threw a faint yellow glow – not much more than that as it was running low on fuel. She broke into a run, her eyes fixed on the square of light that was the front door of the main bungalow.

13

Slow-Burning Fire

Miss White insisted.

"I would like to give Bella her normal lessons this morning," she said when she knocked at the bungalow door shortly before breakfast the following morning. "Changed circumstances don't mean that her education needs to be . . ." She searched for the right word, and settled on "disrupted". That was accompanied by a look of reproach in an otherwise bland countenance.

"You really don't need to bother," said Virginia. "And I wish you'd . . . you'd reconsider. I hate the thought of your leaving so quickly."

But Miss White insisted. Turning away, she said to Virginia, "I shall be in the schoolroom at eight-thirty, as normal. If you could please tell Bella to bring her geography book, we shall do rivers of the world."

Virginia watched the governess retreat over the lawn, back to her own bungalow. She sighed. The situation, she knew, was beyond rescue, but she wondered how she had allowed it to get to this point. Before Miss White arrived, even if their life had been dull, it had nevertheless been straightforward. She had managed Bella's home-schooling well enough, she thought; any deficiencies could quickly be ironed out once she started her proper education back in Scotland. Her reading was good by any standards – certainly it was better than Richard's, and he had the benefit of having been at the Hill School. Her numbers were a little bit shaky – Virginia was uncertain when, and how, they should be tackling long division, but once again a real school would presumably take long division in its stride. Perhaps it would have been wiser not to have a governess at all – nobody else seemed to bother, although she believed that there were one or two families in Colombo – wealthy mercantile families – who had somebody from home to help look after the children and do something about education.

No, it was all Miss White's fault. It was her conduct that had raised suspicions; she must have given Henry some encouragement, if it really was true that he had shown that sort of interest in her. Those things did not come from nowhere, she told herself – a certain coquettishness, even from a plain woman like Miss White, could start a slow-burning fire in a man . . . A slow-burning fire: she had come across that expression in one of the books that she read in private – that is, of the kind that she would never want members of the reading circle to know that she read. It had a slightly lurid cover and was a romance in which all the men, as far as she could make out, were subject to slow-burning fires of one sort or another. It was all rather absurd, really, but she had found herself drawn into it and had ended up turning the pages quickly in her eagerness to find out what happened. None of the slow-burning fires had been extinguished – even by the simpering passivity of the heroines – and at the end there had been what struck her as a general conflagration. But the phrase had stayed with her, and now she found herself thinking, *Men have slow-burning fires within them*. And that included Henry . . . But she stopped herself. If anybody should know about what went on inside Henry, it was she. And she had seen no signs of a slow-burning fire, although was she really sure about that? Another phrase she had encountered in the slow-burning fire book was *married to a stranger.* One of the characters had discovered that her husband had been leading a parallel life, about the details of which she had been completely ignorant. She had woken up and discovered that she was married to a stranger – an expression that was perhaps rather more worrying than any talk about slow-burning fires. Was she married to a stranger? Was there a side to Henry that she had not yet discovered and that she would never be able to touch? Men could be elusive – she knew that; they could withhold themselves; they could remain private in a way in which women found more difficult to do themselves. You could never be absolutely sure of what was going on in a man's head, however much you thought you understood him. And that thought was worrying, however one approached it. It was perfectly possible that Henry was passionately in love with Miss White – unlikely though that might seem; it was perfectly possible that Miss White had not only allowed that but had encouraged it because she had never before had a man fall for her – in spite of her ridiculous claim the night before of having had many lovers. Many lovers! Miss White, with her caked-on rouge and her preoccupation with rivers of the world and French verbs? That was laughable. And yet, laughable things happened all the time. Ceylon was full of stories of unbelievable, laughable things in which the wrong people – the entirely wrong people – had the last laugh. So it was entirely possible that Miss White had said to Henry, "We must get rid of your wife," and he had said, "It will be easy for her to have an unfortunate fall." It is possible that when that did not work, Miss White had suggested something else that could never be laid at anybody's door – a snake bite – and had then found one of those itinerant snake charmers that you occasionally saw in Kandy, with their baskets of cobras. She had seen this on several occasions and recoiled in disgust – she did not like snakes at all – but presumably these snake charmers could be tempted by a large enough payment to use one of their snakes to get rid of somebody. Far stranger things had happened, she thought. There had been that man in Colombo who had drugged his wife with opium with the specific aim of getting her addicted and then abandoning her for his lover. And the poor woman had ended up in an opium den somewhere, unable to get away from the clutches of the drug. Somebody had said that was a true story, although others had said that it was entirely false and had been made up by one of the men in the bar at the club when the conversation had lagged a bit.

She made an effort to remove these thoughts firmly from her mind. Henry loved her. Henry would never do anything like that. She should be careful: allowing oneself to dwell on such matters was a sure way to become unbalanced. If she continued to think in that way, then she would end up half mad. You had to be careful. This beguiling country, with its hills and its skies, and its vegetation, so green and intense that it could drive you crazy – it had happened before, and it would happen again. She would not let it happen to her.

And so when Henry returned at noon, she greeted him with a smile and with the suggestion that they sit on the veranda together, he with a cold beer and she with a shandy, while he told her about the dinner in Colombo. He would regale her with stories about the people whom he knew down there – people in whom she had no real interest – but she would be attentive and would laugh at all the right places, and they would be happy, as they always had been, in their particular, not very dramatic way.

He was happy to do this, although he wanted to have a quick bath beforehand, to wash off the dust of the journey. That done, he appeared on the veranda smelling of the sandalwood soap he liked to use in his bath, a smell that she would forever associate with him, she thought – with this place in the clouds, with this time in her life.

"Where's Bella?"

"With Miss White."

He took a sip of his beer. "Lovely," he said, referring to the ice-cold beer and the feel of the condensation on the side of the glass. He always loved that.

And she took a sip of her shandy – three parts lemonade and one part beer, a drink that she found suitable for lunchtime when gin would be far too strong and would effectively ruin the afternoon. "Rivers of the world," she said. "Miss White has spent the morning teaching her about rivers of the world. And some other things too, I think. She said they'd finish by lunchtime."

"Poor Bella," said Henry. "Rivers of the world – does she really need to know quite so much about them? I suppose one ought to have a vague idea where the Amazon is, and the Ganges, and so on. But beyond that . . ."

Virginia shrugged. "She thinks it important." She changed the subject. She would have to say something more about Miss White's change of plans, but she did not want to broach the subject just yet.

"And the dinner?" she asked.

He laughed. "Oh, the dinner. Just as I expected. Speech after speech. One old boy droned on for twenty-eight minutes – I timed him – and then stood up afterwards to say that he had something to add. The groans could be heard from one end of the room to the other. He was too deaf to notice."

"Well, you did your duty."

He nodded. "There was a book that they asked everybody to sign. That was to check up, I think, on who was shirking. I'm glad I went. These government types, you know, have long memories. They chalk it all up."

She reached for her shandy and was taking a sip when she heard a voice from within the house.

"That's Bella's lesson finished." She lowered her glass. She would have to tell him before Bella appeared – or Miss White did, for that matter, although now she saw Miss White making her way back across the lawn to her bungalow. She would be preparing her lunch, she thought, and would eat on her own veranda, out of sight of the main house. She felt saddened at the thought of this lonely woman, eating by herself: had they failed in their duty of hospitality? Had they made her feel isolated and alone, far away from any friends or relatives, cooped up in this remote place?

She thought that Bella was probably in her room, playing, as she liked to do, after her lessons. She would only appear when the bell for lunch went – which meant that now there was time.

"There's been a development," she began. "She's going early."

"Who?"

"Miss White."

She had not intended to watch for his reaction, but she could not help but do so. She saw him frown – almost imperceptibly – but then the frown disappeared, and he said, quite evenly, "Any reason?"

Virginia hesitated. She was not sure what to say. She could not reveal what Bella had done because that would amount to a confession of suspicion – even if not to an outright accusation. Yet she did not want to tell a barefaced lie; she had never deceived him – actively, that is – and she had no desire to do so now.

"Oh, some little misunderstanding over a chance remark from Bella." And then, glossing over this as quickly as she could, she went on, "She's more sensitive than one might imagine, you know. On the outside she's all very brisk and schoolmistressy, but there are things going on underneath that exterior."

He gave a start. "Things? Such as?"

She waved a hand in the air. "She broods on things, I suspect. You know how some people dissect every little remark that others make and try to work out what it means – to see whether there's an agenda. You know how some people are."

"You mean paranoia?"

"Not quite. That's a bit extreme, isn't it? I don't imagine she thinks people are out to get her. That's what paranoia is, isn't it?"

"Something like that."

"Well, she's not like that. But she's a bit . . . how shall I put it? A bit prickly? A bit on her dignity?"

He thought about this. "She's sensitive, I think. Women often are."

She looked at him. "More sensitive than other women. Is that what you're saying?"

He shook his head. "I didn't say that. It's just that sometimes one has to watch what you say – especially if you're a man. You say something that can be taken quite the wrong way."

"And men don't do that? They don't take things the wrong way?"

He shrugged. "Some do. But most men . . ." He smiled.

"We're an uncomplicated breed, you know. We say what we think we mean, and we assume that what other people say is, well, just that – what they say. We don't always look for hidden meaning."

She was relieved that the conversation had drifted away from what Bella might have said. "Anyway," she continued, "she's leaving tomorrow. Or so she said. I told her there was no hurry, but she had the bit between her teeth. She seemed to think . . ." She trailed off.

He waited. "Yes?"

"She seemed to think that I took a dim view of her."

He reached for his beer. She watched his hand. It was steady. This was not a man discussing his lover with his wife. She felt reassured.

He did not look at her as he spoke. "Odd that she should say that."

She glanced at him, and then quickly looked away. "And we had a bit of a scare. A snake."

It seemed as if he had not heard her. "You haven't given her any reason to think that you . . ." He hesitated, waving a hand vaguely, almost dismissively, ". . . that you don't get on with her, have you?"

She did not answer, but returned to the subject of the snake. It occurred to her that she should have told him about this earlier – the moment he had arrived back. It would have been more natural to do it then – more the act of a woman who trusted her husband – which she did, of course; she trusted him, she told herself; she wanted to trust him. "There was a snake. It was in the pavilion. Bella was there."

He frowned. It was as if he was returning from some distant place. "In the pavilion?"

"Yes, in the basket I keep the magazines in. Inside it, I believe."

He looked puzzled. "Odd." And then he said, "What was it? I saw a pipe snake down there not all that long ago. Odd little thing. Completely harmless, of course."

"A cobra."

There was no mistaking his surprise. "My God. Inside the basket?"

"Yes."

He shuddered. "But that could have been dreadful." He made a face. "What's a cobra doing up here? They don't like cool weather."

That had occurred to her, too, she told him. "Miss White saw it too, thank heavens." That was hardly a full acknowledgement of what Miss White had done, she thought.

He did not seem interested in this detail. "I'll get the men to cut the grass back. The grass at the sides is a bit high. If we cut it back it should discourage any nasties." He paused. "And everybody was all right?"

"We were a bit shocked."

"I'm sure you were."

She took a sip of her shandy. Suddenly it seemed too sweet, and she wondered whether perhaps her tastes were changing. The older women, those who had been married to planters for decades, ending up drinking spirits at lunchtime. There was a group of them at the club – who sat and chatted over gin-and-French on Saturdays, their voices rising, sometimes shrieking with laughter at some particularly malicious scrap of gossip. She would never end up like that. They would go home well before either of them reached that stage. They should go home now, she thought. She should bring pressure to bear on Henry to give up while they still had a marriage and before they became like the rest of them. This was not their place, and sooner or later they would be shown the door; why wait? They were itching to do that in India, and the same would happen here, even if the voices here were less strident and more accepting of the compromises and juggling dreamed up to keep the system going. She sighed inwardly; that was not her problem. It never was the woman's problem, was it? Women were left to provide support, to shore things up, while men took the decisions with the chess board on which everybody was put out like pieces in a game.

He was looking at her quizzically, as well he might, she thought, because had she explained to him what she was thinking, he would have been dumbfounded. He had not questioned any of this, she believed. It had never occurred to him that any of this was unusual, even, let alone actually wrong. And there was a reason for that, of course: there was tea to be planted and harvested. Who was going to do that if he, and others like him, were not prepared to live this lonely existence, so far from home? Nobody had done it before, and if they left, she was not sure who would do it in their place.

He had said something to her, which she had not heard, and now he repeated himself. "You were miles away. I asked whether Bella has been told that Miss White is going early?"

She nodded.

"And?" he asked.

She shrugged. "I don't think it matters to her one way or the other. She knows she's going home. She's excited about school."

It was her moment, and she suddenly decided to seize it. "I'd like to go too."

He was staring at his feet. "You? With Bella?"

"Yes. I'm sorry to spring this on you. We should have talked before this."

He looked up. "Then why didn't we?"

She met his gaze, and the reproach it conveyed. She felt a momentary resentment. "A conversation involves two people, Henry. Two. If you don't have two, then it becomes a monologue. It's one person talking to herself. It's not a conversation."

"I wasn't blaming you," he said, grudgingly. "I should have talked too."

"Well, we didn't."

He sighed. "And now we are." He paused. "Better late than never, I suppose."

He looked at her, and she saw that there was tenderness in his gaze. "It can't be easy," he continued. "It can't be easy for women – sending their children off like that."

"I hate the thought," she said. "I hate the thought of it. I always have. Right from the first day you have the child, you think: I'm going to have to give this up. That's what you think. And then you think: well, I can have another one, and another one after that, and keep somebody in the nest for years that way, until a reckoning that's far enough away that you can stop thinking about it."

He was listening. She was unburdening herself in a way in which she had not done before, and he was listening. It had never occurred to her that he would sit there and listen, and not raise objections to these destabilising thoughts, these female thoughts that lapped at the edges of his male world and would wash it all away if given the chance.

Suddenly he reached for her hand. "Oh, Virgie." It was his pet name for her – not used very often, but brought out in real tenderness. "I know. I know how you feel. And I feel a bit like that myself. I feel all . . ." He broke off. There was pain in his eyes.

She returned the pressure of his hand. It was as if they were shaking hands: two newly introduced strangers, shaking hands.

"You really want to go, don't you?"

She nodded. She was going to cry. She felt the tears coming, and she knew that she would not be able to resist. They were coming from behind a dam, somewhere in the up-country of her feelings, and they would not be kept in.

"All right," he said. "You should go."

"And you?"

He looked at her. She tried to make out what his expression meant, but she could not fathom it. It seemed to her that he was struggling with something within himself.

At last he spoke. "I'll come too."

She found it hard to take it in, and for a moment the tears were forgotten. "You mean that you'll come with me? We'll all go?"

He confirmed that this was what he had been thinking. They would all go home, although Bella might precede them, since arrangements had been made, and it would take months before he could extricate himself from the estate. Bella would need to start school, he felt, and they could not delay that much longer.

She struggled. "You'll sell this place?"

"Yes, I'll sell this place. In fact . . ."

She waited. She felt exhilarated. She could give him all the time he needed to tell her whatever he had in mind. The important thing was that the decision had been made.

"In fact," he continued, "I called in on Pessoa down in Colombo. He happened to mention that there was somebody looking around for something. Somebody who had been up in Assam and had a bit of spare money to invest."

She was excited. "You could sell to him," she said. "Perfect."

He laughed. "You can't just sell to the first person who comes along."

"Why not?"

He seemed surprised. "Because you're selling more than just . . . well, more than just a couple of bungalows and a factory and so on. You're selling a whole world up here. There are all these people . . ." He gestured towards the hillside where the lines were – the houses, the families.

She was chastened. "Of course. Of course."

"I'd want to make sure that whoever I sold up to treated my people decently."

She knew that. He was a decent man. And she felt ashamed to have thought the things that she had thought; she felt ashamed to have mistrusted him. There were plenty of women who were married to men they could not – and should not – trust, but she was not one of them.

Now he asked, "What arrangements has Miss White made?"

She replied, "She wasn't very specific. As I told you, she was very cool towards me."

He looked concerned. "I'm going to have a word with her."

Virginia was worried. "About what? I don't think she's going to change her mind."

He conceded that that was unlikely, but he would still want to offer help with whatever needed to be done. "She'll need to get down to Colombo."

"She has friends in Kandy. I think she was planning to go to them in the first place. Then down to Colombo. Presumably she'll then just pick up her original plan a few days later."

He rose to his feet and looked across the lawn towards Miss White's bungalow. "I'll go and see her."

She rose too. "I'll come with you."

He shook his head. "No. You stay. I'll just be a minute. It's probably easier for me . . ."

But why? She did not understand why it should be easier for him to talk to Miss White. She opened her mouth to say something, but he had reached the steps down from the veranda and was on his way. She watched him for a few moments as he strode across the lawn, and then she turned and went into the house, into the corridor, with its cool air and its dark silences. She passed the open door of the living room and saw a letter lying on her writing table. She needed to address the envelope and look for a stamp, and she did this now. Drifting down the corridor there came the sound of Bella singing in her room. Virginia loved that and listened now to the song that Miss White had taught Bella when she had first arrived, 'Sur le Pont d'Avignon'. It had rapidly become Bella's favourite, and they heard it at odd times – from the garden, from the bathroom, from the schoolroom itself. Why did they dance on the Avignon bridge? She had once almost come to the point of asking Miss White that but had not done so in the end, afraid of being shown up as ignorant. It might be that everyone knew why this was and that she, alone, was puzzled. She did not want to give Miss White that opportunity to parade her superior education. "Why do they dance? But don't you know that they *always* danced on that bridge in Avignon?"

She went into the living room. Henry called it the drawing room; she did that too, when talking to him, but otherwise referred to it as the living room. He said, "You don't need euphemisms, you know" – and laughed. "Or affectations," she replied. "This is a bungalow." He came from a slightly higher echelon of society than she did, although she thought, in her heart, that these divisions were irrelevant – and unkind. We are all simply walking bags of organs, she said to herself. Heart, lungs, miles of piping – larger, and more ruthlessly calculating, versions of the monkeys that infested the trees at the edge of the lawn – and yet we clothed ourselves in gradations and niceties and superstitions about how you did what. There was a woman at the club who was the niece of a man who had been knighted for donations to a political party, and who thought, quite seriously, that this made her somehow better than the rest of them. The absurdity of this amused Virginia but seemed to escape others, who deferred to her sense of her own superiority.

She sat down at her desk and reached for the fountain pen she had left lying on a large square of blotting paper. She noticed that she had forgotten to replace the cap, and this meant that the ink would have dried in the nib. She would probably have to run it under the tap for a second or two to dislodge the coagulation – if ink actually coagulates, she thought, or was it only blood that did that?

And she was thinking that when she heard the shot. It was quick and sharp, but it brought with it what seemed like a brief and tiny echo. And then silence.

There was a screeching of monkeys from the trees outside. It was as if they were scandalised.

She pushed the chair out from behind her. It toppled over. Bella came running up the corridor. Virginia gasped. Bella stood in the door. She had Li Po in her right hand. He was being held by his arm – his good arm – but he was twisted and was gazing intently at the floor.

Bella looked at her as if expecting her mother to explain what had happened. Then she said, "Has Daddy shot a monkey? Has he?"

14

It Was an Accident, Nothing More

By the time Virginia reached the veranda, Henry was striding across the lawn towards the bungalow. He waved a hand, half in greeting, half in a gesture that said, *Don't worry*. She watched him and was aware that Bella had wrapped her arms around her waist. She bent down and patted her on the shoulder, not sure what to say, but then deciding, "Daddy's all right, darling. See. See Daddy."

Now he reached them, and he was smiling. "Nothing to worry about. *Alles in Ordnung*." He sometimes said *alles in Ordnung* to make them laugh. It was a pet expression that he had picked up from a man who had worked for years on the family farm in the Borders. He had been captured by the Germans in 1916 and had taken two years to learn his few words of German. "That was the only German he picked up," Henry said. "He was not a great linguist."

She began to speak. Her voice sounded too high-pitched. She swallowed, and started again. "What happened?"

He glanced down at Bella, and then back at his wife. "Nothing happened. Nothing."

Bella let go of Virginia. "Did you shoot something?"

He shook his head. "Oh, that. No, that wasn't me shooting anything." He tried to laugh, but Virginia could tell that he was tense, and the laugh withered on the vine.

"It was an accident," he said.

She closed her eyes. This was simply not happening. He had shot her. Henry had shot Miss White and was claiming it was an accident.

He was addressing her. "Virginia? Are you . . . Darling, nothing's happened. Everybody's fine."

She opened her eyes once again. She saw Li Po staring up at her. Chinese poets had seen worse than this; they saw some terrible things up in the mountains, in their exile.

"Yes," he said, reaching forward to tousle Bella's hair. "Miss White was putting her revolver away, and it went off. She needs to learn about safety catches, I fear."

Virginia breathed a sigh of relief. "You see," she said to Bella. "Everything's all right. Daddy didn't shoot one of the poor monkeys."

He laughed now, more credibly. "Not that they don't deserve it – some of those are rascals."

She saw him put a hand into his pocket, and she suddenly realised that he was concealing the revolver. He noticed the direction of her gaze and said, "I'm looking after it for her."

Bella asked, "Is that Miss White's gun?"

"It is," he said. "She won't be needing it in Colombo, will she? You don't need a gun in Colombo."

And at this point Miss White came out onto her veranda.

"There she is," said Henry. "She said she was going to go for a walk before lunch."

Virginia looked across the lawn. The governess was standing by her front door, staring across the lawn. Virginia raised a hand to wave, but Miss White turned round and went back inside, as might one who was in a sulk.

"Go and wash your hands for lunch," Henry said to

Bella. "Go on, now. You don't want to eat your lunch with dirty hands."

Bella obeyed, although reluctantly. She glanced at her father as she did so, a glance of reproach. He smiled back at her, pretending not to notice.

Virginia stayed with Henry. As soon as Bella had gone, she whispered to him, "What happened?"

"I told you," he said. "The revolver went off accidentally. These things . . . These things happen."

She stared at him. "Henry, are you telling me the truth?"

This might have been expected to anger him, but he simply answered, "Of course I am. Are you suggesting that she tried to shoot me? Is that what you're saying?"

She did not know what to say. She was suggesting that, unless . . . She hardly dared imagine the alternative.

"I'll tell you exactly what happened," said Henry. "I knocked on the door, and I thought I heard her say come in. I thought I did. Perhaps I didn't – I don't know. Sometimes you think you hear things that you don't actually hear."

"Of course."

"Well, there you are. I went in, and she was standing next to a suitcase that she had put on her sofa. She was packing things away. She turned round. She had some clothing in her hands, I think – I didn't pay much attention to it, though, and then the gun went off. It was a terrible shock. I wasn't expecting it."

"No." It was all she could think of to say.

"She was as surprised as I was, I think. She screamed, and I thought, *Oh, my God, she's shot herself.* But then she was still standing, and I realised that it had been fired accidentally. I said something to her. I don't know what it was. I probably said, *You stupid woman* or something like that. That was what I was thinking, I'm afraid; I don't know.

Maybe not. But I went up to the case and took the gun. It was lying on a cardigan. I took it, you see, because I thought that if you don't know how to operate a safety catch, then you have no business having a weapon in your possession. Basic stuff. I told her that I was going to put it in the safe up at the office."

He stopped. Suddenly he looked shocked, and she realised that the calm demeanour had been a front. As he looked at her, his lip quivered slightly. One would not have noticed it if one was not looking for it, but she did see it now, and she put her arms around him.

"My poor darling. What a . . . What a shock. A shock for you."

"Nothing," he said. "All over now. All over." He nodded and then moved away from her, freeing himself of her embrace. "We need to have lunch," he said, and then added, "After these events I find I have a bit of an appetite."

He still had his hand in his pocket, holding the revolver.

"You must put that thing away," she said.

He looked down. "Of course. I'll go and lock it up."

He turned round, and she made her way into the dining room, where she rang a bell. Michael appeared.

"Soup is ready," he said.

"Good."

He lingered before going back into the kitchen, and she realised that he was hoping for some explanation.

"There was an accident," she said. "Nothing bad. A gun went off by mistake. Miss White's gun. Nobody has been hurt."

He nodded. "Guns no good," he muttered.

"No. No good at all." And as he left, she added, "I hope the soup is not too spicy, Michael."

It would be, she thought; of course it would be too spicy. But the cook simply grinned and said with complete sincerity, "No, no. Not too spicy. Just right, Lady."

Part II

In Scotland, in 1952

I

Matthew Arnold

Bella enrolled in the University of St Andrews in 1949, at the age of nineteen, moving into a shared room in Wardlaw, part of University Hall, where woman undergraduates had lived since the late nineteenth century. Wardlaw was a Scots baronial mansion, a building of turrets and castellations, a place of winding staircases and impractical spaces. The students were tucked into sparsely furnished rooms that were too cold in the winter and too windy in the summer. Each had two small desks, a shared wardrobe, and two uncomfortable single beds. They were softened by the cushions that the students brought with them from home, and by the rugs they purchased from a soft-furnishings store in the town.

On her second day in the university, Bella sat at her desk, writing her name in the books she had ordered from the bookshop in South Street, and paging through the synopses of the courses for which she had enrolled. Later that day she was to attend a lecture on Matthew Arnold. Her roommate, Anne, who was studying French, was to have her first language class.

Anne, who was English and had been brought up in London, said to her, "So you've lived all your life in Edinburgh?"

Bella shook her head. "No. Most of it, though, I suppose. Since I was nine."

"And before that?"

Bella put down the copy of *Chambers Dictionary* in which she had just inscribed her name. "Before that I lived in Ceylon. I came back to go to school here in Scotland." She re-opened the *Chambers* and ran a finger down the list of words. "Gressorial," she read. "You don't know what that is, I imagine."

Anne smiled. "And neither did you – until a moment ago."

"True. Adapted for walking, apparently. It says here it's a zoological term."

Anne looked out of the window. "It's much colder here than in London. I don't know if I've brought enough woollens. My mother warned me." She turned to look at Bella. "Did yours?"

"Did mine what?"

"Did your mother fuss around like a broody hen? Did she tell you what you should bring with you to university?"

Bella stared at the page of *Chambers*.

The silence lasted long enough for Anne to realise her mistake. She reddened. "I'm sorry," she stuttered. "Your mother isn't . . . dead, is she? I'm really sorry if I've . . ."

Bella looked up from the dictionary. "You weren't to know. Don't worry, anyway. It was quite a long time ago – during the War. 1942."

Anne lowered her voice. "I see. We knew lots of people who died in the Blitz. I had an aunt who was killed. And a cousin too."

"It was nothing to do with that," said Bella. "Nothing to do with London. They were still in Ceylon. I was sent back in 1939, just before the War, and they stayed."

"So you came back all by yourself?"

"With a friend of my mother's. Then I went to my aunt."

"And your parents?"

"They were meant to come a little later – my father was selling the tea estate, you see, but the sale fell through because of the War."

"It changed everybody's lives. My father never really got over it. He's somewhere . . ." She waved a hand airily. "He's somewhere in the desert still. In North Africa. Not physically, of course, but inside him. He talks about it all the time."

Bella said that she supposed it was a big thing for everybody. "If you thought you were going to die, then life must have been . . . Well, I can't imagine what it must have been like."

Anne looked grave. "He cries sometimes. I've seen him. When he has whisky, usually." She smiled. "I suppose that's understandable."

Bella continued with her story. "They had to stay, you see – my parents – and they were still there when the Japanese bombed Ceylon."

Anne winced. "Oh no . . ."

"It was my parents' bad luck that they had gone down to Colombo to see some friends just a day or two before the Japanese raid. The house they were staying in took a direct hit."

Anne watched her. "I'm really sorry."

"Thank you. I suppose they didn't know anything about it."

"And you were back here?"

"Yes, in Edinburgh. I was staying with an aunt. She lives there. I was already in school, and so I carried on with that. My aunt became my guardian. She was kind to me – she still is."

Anne looked down at her hands. "But I imagine it's not the same – not quite the same thing . . ." She stopped herself once more, appalled at her own lack of tact. "I mean . . ."

"I loved Ceylon," said Bella.

Relieved, Anne said, "I know somebody who lived in India. Same thing, more or less, isn't it? She came back to this country – well, England, I suppose, not Scotland, for school. She was always talking about India and the things she did there. She missed it."

"I did. I cried for days when I first came to Edinburgh. I was homesick, I suppose. Then I got used to it, and the memory of what my life had been like there faded. And after my parents died, I put it out of my mind, really."

Anne waited for her to say more, but Bella became silent. Then she said, "Now this."

"You mean St Andrews?"

Bella nodded. "Yes."

Anne had been lying on her bed as they talked. Now she stood up. "I'm determined to be happy. I'm determined."

"Me too."

"And find a boyfriend."

Bella laughed. "Me too."

"Not any old boyfriend, of course."

"Of course not."

Anne noticed something. She pointed to the small bookcase that Bella had beside her desk on the other side of the room. On the bottom shelf were Li Po and Po Chü-i.

"Have you just put those there? Those dolls?"

Bella smiled. "They were in my trunk. I've had them all my life. I thought that would be a good place for them."

"They're lovely. They really are."

"Thank you."

"They're good enough to be in a museum."

"Perhaps. But I'd never give them away. Never."

"Of course not."

She went to her lecture on Arnold, the first in the course in Victorian literature which she had chosen from the limited list on offer. There would be three lectures a week, they were told, and a tutorial in a small group of six students and a tutor. Her tutor was to be an Australian in his late twenties, who had completed a doctorate in Cambridge. He had been offered a chair in Melbourne, rumour had it, or if not an actual chair, a position that could in a short time become a chair. "He knows everything there is to know about Coleridge. He's writing a book on him. Two books, in fact." That was what the students who had been tutored by him the previous year said amongst themselves. Bella was prepared to be in awe of him but was immediately struck by his conceit. His gaze rested on her, and lingered, but she turned away.

The professor in charge of the course was the author of a book on Wordsworth she had seen displayed in the university bookshop under a *Highly Recommended* sign. She had toyed with the idea of buying it, and had almost done so, but had been put off by the price and the density of the text. But now he was standing before them, at the podium, in his black gown, a man in his sixties somewhere, she thought, slightly stooped, in a scholarly way, and beginning to address them on the questioning of faith that followed Darwin's discoveries.

"It's all in 'Dover Beach'," he said. "Which, I take it, most, if not all of you, have read." He paused, smiling wryly. "Or perhaps not. One should never assume that the people to whom one is talking are of the same mind as oneself. And of course, when I use the term *of the same mind* I mean not only *of the same opinion*, but having, so to speak, the same *furniture* in their mind."

There was a ripple of laughter. The young man seated next to Bella adjusted his tie nervously. He whispered to her, "I've read *nothing*. Nothing at all. Have you read this 'Dover Beach' thing?"

She nodded. She had read it in her English class in her final year at school in Edinburgh. The English teacher loved Arnold and made them read the poem aloud, pausing to discuss what each line meant.

"I'm so ignorant," said the young man, behind a cupped hand.

"We all are," she whispered back. "That's why we've come to university."

"The central notion," the professor continued, "is that there is – or was – a sea of faith that girdled the world. It was the guiding principle, the thing that kept humanity together – not that humanity was really together in the sense of being in some sort of voluntary association. Guiding principles – whether or not they be faiths – have a habit of keeping people *down* rather than *together* – if I make my meaning clear.

"The building was a massive one – a whole construction of assumptions and conventions: a vast roof, like the roof of Hagia Sophia in Istanbul, under which variety and difference and experience of every persuasion was gathered, and made subservient. An unruly, awkward world, with all its cruelties and darkness, was subsumed under this overarching system of belief in the perfectibility of mankind. Imagine that. My metaphor is an architectural one; Arnold, though, was using metaphors of the natural world – the movement of tides, light, darkness. And then, suddenly, the sea withdraws – the poet hears it – and the lonely, rocky shore is exposed. The sea of faith might normally cover that, but now it seems to have withdrawn, and in its place there is emptiness and doubt.

"Arnold, you see, was well ahead of his time – preternaturally so. He predicted what we would come to feel in the twentieth century when we reached the unsettling conclusion that in the absence of faith we are on our own and that there are no reassuring and authoritative answers – no single set of beliefs that can make sense of it all. The dissolution of empires, both spiritual and temporal, was what followed from that. Faith was a luxury that only the determined, the inventive and the irretrievably ignorant could afford: for the rest of us, there was the loneliness of doubt or the bleak knowledge that there was no ultimate justice, no irrefutable right and wrong, no graspable meaning in a random and sometimes uncomfortable universe."

She glanced at the young man beside her. He smiled back at her. "You see," he whispered.

She wrote to her aunt in Edinburgh every week, telling her about the lectures she attended, about the chaperoned tea parties in University Hall, about Anne's description of her language classes. Her aunt wrote back once a month, usually on a postcard, telling her that life in Edinburgh was very dull without her and were it not for her membership of her Highland Fiddle Orchestra, a collection of almost fifty amateur fiddlers devoted to playing Scottish music, there would be little to write about.

Then at the end of her first month in St Andrews, Bella wrote:

> I must tell you about a discovery I have made. It was very surprising for me – something I should, perhaps, have been aware of, but that I had simply not thought of. You must know the sort of thing I'm talking

about. Something that is right under your nose and that you should discover, but that you don't.

You remember that I had a governess in Ceylon before I came back to Scotland. I think I showed you a photograph of her once – it was in that album that Mummy gave me before I left. And there were some photographs of her, too, in the papers that the people in Colombo sent over with Daddy's things after the War. She was that tall, rather skinny woman, who is in the photograph of Mummy and me sitting in the pavilion that we had at the edge of the garden. It was a bit like a summer-house, right on the edge of a steep drop. Mummy fell from it once – I think I told you about that – but wasn't badly hurt because a tree broke her fall.

Anyway, she's that woman – the woman in the photo. She was called Miss White, and she was with us for over a year. Then she went away just before I was sent home. I don't know what happened to her, as there was a bit of a row, and she never wrote to me nor to Mummy. We weren't quite sure where she went. She said that she was going to go to Calcutta because she had friends there and she wanted to see them again. She used to tell us that she knew some very grand people there, but Mummy was not sure whether that was quite true. I was too young to know much about that.

She was Scottish too, although she had gone to boarding school in England. She used to talk about that sometimes, but I can't remember what she said. That's not to say that I don't remember some of the things she said – I do. She talked a lot of French to me, and she was very keen on geography. We spent a lot of time learning about mountains and rivers. I still know a lot about famous rivers, and will tell anybody all about them if asked. But nobody asks, which is just as well, I suppose, as I wouldn't want to spend too much time with people who could only talk about the Nile and so on. (That's a joke, by the way, as I'm sure you realise!)

She crossed out the last sentence: her aunt had a sharp sense of humour – for an aunt – and it seemed condescending to flag up one's jokes, as if the recipient lacked the understanding to appreciate them. And then she realised that striking through words merely draws attention to them, so she abandoned the page in question and started a new one.

There's a professor here who teaches English literature. We enjoy his lectures, although sometimes he loses us a bit. He is some sort of authority on Matthew Arnold and on Wordsworth, on whom he's written a book. I almost bought it when I was in the bookshop on my very first day here in St Andrews. I picked it up and paged through it. There were three hundred pages, and I decided that I would not buy it because I was not at all sure that I would want to read three hundred pages about Wordsworth. One hundred pages, maybe, but three hundred . . . Anyway, when I started going to his lectures, I thought I might get the book after all. I've never known anybody who's written a book. Do you know anybody? Of course you do: you told me that you knew Compton Mackenzie a bit and that you sometimes saw him walking about Drummond Place. Everybody says that *Whisky Galore* is the funniest book there is, but I haven't read it yet. Perhaps I shall read it when I've had enough Matthew Arnold and Wordsworth.

I went back to the bookshop yesterday to buy the Wordsworth book because I felt guilty that here I was at university at last and was too lazy to read three-hundred-page books and also because I thought that if my professor was prepared to go to all the trouble of writing a book about Wordsworth then the very least I could do would be to read it. It had been on a table that they have near the cashier's desk, but when I went to find it there was no sign of it. Where it had been there was a large book on the history of golf! That had the same sign that I had seen next to the Wordsworth book – the sign that said *Highly Recommended*. I think they just put that sign next to any book that they want people to buy, whether or not they've read it.

I asked them whether they had a copy, and they said that they had sold five copies of it since the term began and that they thought that everybody who went to his lectures was now buying it. They said that this sometimes happened, as students liked to quote their professors' books back to them in the examinations and get better marks as a result. They said that was a well-known trick, and it all went to show that professors were just as vain as the rest of us! They asked me if I would like them to order a copy for me, but I said no. I was worried that if I said yes, they would think I was one of those students who wanted to impress their professors, and that I wasn't the type who would normally read about Wordsworth. I know you shouldn't worry about what other people think about you, but I do, I'm afraid.

The point about all this is the professor's name. He's called Professor James Alfred White, or J.A. White, as it says on the cover of the book. It took me a while to realise it, but then I remembered something. Miss White said that her father was a university professor, and I remember her saying something about St Andrews. She also read Wordsworth to me – she made me learn that poem about daffodils that *everyone* has to learn – and she said that her father liked it. I distinctly remembered her saying that. Now surely there are not going to be two Professor Whites who are keen on Wordsworth, and so I think he – my professor, that is – is Miss White's father. It is an amazing coincidence to be taught by a daughter and then by her father. I should ask him about her, I suppose, but I don't want to bother him. And I haven't heard from her since those days, and I doubt if she wants to hear from me. In fact, I'm sure she won't want to hear from me.

She concluded the letter with a few anecdotes about the other young women in University Hall, including a story of one who had been given a car by her wealthy parents and had then lent it to her newly acquired boyfriend. He had driven it into the sea one evening after a party, and it was now ruined. That had been the talk of the university for days, she said, and the young man in question was going to be fined by the University as well as be asked to pay for the damage to the car, which he could ill afford. It was rumoured that he was going to join the navy as the only way out of his difficulties. Naval officers were always doing things like that, people said, and so they would not mind too much.

She posted the letter and went into a tearoom on North Street, where she was planning to meet Anne. Anne had been working on an assignment on Arthur Rimbaud. She confessed to being in love with the work of the poet. "He must have been such a romantic figure," she enthused.

"Didn't Rimbaud shoot Verlaine? Or was it Verlaine who shot Rimbaud?"

"Verlaine. He shot Rimbaud after an argument. He hit him in the wrist. Another shot missed. He went to prison for two years, where he wrote thirty-two poems." Anne paused. "Rimbaud was a bit bad, I agree. But all the best poets are a bit bad, don't you think?"

Bella thought that Matthew Arnold probably was not – nor was Wordsworth – and so she said that she wondered whether that was an observation that only rang true when applied to French poets. English poets were far too high-minded and respectable to be bad in that way and concentrated more on the sea of faith and daffodils and other subjects on which it was hard to be convincingly dissolute, although one might be able to manage it if one really tried.

Waiting for her friend, a cup of tea and a buttered scone in front of her, she found herself thinking of Professor White and of Miss White herself. For the first few years following the raid on Ceylon, the loss of her parents had seemed strangely unreal to her, the news of their death merging into memories of war-time news broadcasts of battles, retreats, engagements in foreign theatres of war – footage in the cinema newsreels that she had watched, with her aunt and a cousin, in the news cinema on Princes Street. It was as if their loss were some sort of Pathé News event, accompanied by the stirring music that was the soundtrack to shots of tanks rolling across plains, of jeeps of soldiery entering liberated Italian villages. She had grieved, but in a silent, private way, half believing that it had not happened and that they might somehow be found to have survived, in the way in which so many people, thought to be dead, were turning up, emerging from the throngs of displaced people who made up the human flotsam covering Europe. The reality of what happened came home eventually, and her stunted grief expressed itself, allowing memories of her childhood, and of Ceylon, to come to the fore. She had put all that out of her mind – the bungalow on the hillside, the garden in which she had played, the pavilion on which she had spent those long afternoon hours with her mother, enjoying the cool breeze that wafted up the hillside below, with the *National Geographic* and *The Illustrated London News* and her two dolls. And the outings to the club, where, when her parents were drinking sundowners with the other planters, she and Richard chased fireflies and told one another stories of what they were going to do with their lives, which they felt had not quite started yet, but that would begin when they were in that place called *home* that they both longed for and dreaded, in roughly equal measure. Because *home*, for Richard at least, would be boarding school and the things that happened in boarding school, which they had heard could be horrid, and for her was living with an aunt she had never met and who could, for all she knew, be a strict disciplinarian and not give her enough to eat, as stepmothers were said to do.

Now, as she sat in the tearoom, waiting for her friend, she thought: *I did a terrible thing.* She had written in her letter, *I doubt if she wants to hear from me. In fact, I'm sure she won't want to hear from me.* She had written that without really thinking it through, but it was what she felt. Miss White would not want to hear from her because of what she had done to her. She had caused her to lose her job.

She had done it with all the innocent carelessness of a child, but now the full weight of what she had done came back to her. She had framed Miss White – it was as simple as that. She had framed her.

The dawning of this realisation brought a sudden feeling of hollowness. She felt sickened by what she had done. In so far as she had been aware of it, she had simply repressed the memory of the injustice, and now it came back to her, in vivid detail, even after more than ten years – the hiding of her father's clothing, her silence, her half-hearted attempt to own up, and then her connivance in the getting rid of Miss White. She had done all of this. It was not some other little girl in a distant country long ago; it was *her*. She was the one who had done it to a person who had done her no wrong – who had, in fact, been her teacher, with all that that implied.

She felt her heart beating within her, responding to the bodily reactions that went with guilt. Adrenaline? Or was that the chemical that went with fear? And yet she felt that there must be a chemistry to guilt and self-reproach. Because she had felt its effect, which seemed as real and as potent in its effect as if she had swallowed some powerful drug.

Anne arrived, apologising for being late. "The lecture went on and on. And was very boring, I'm afraid. Perhaps I should switch courses. Divinity, maybe?" She laughed.

"You've still got Rimbaud."

"Yes, there's still Rimbaud."

Anne was looking at her with concern. "You look upset. Has something happened?"

Bella shook her head. "No." And then she said, "Well, maybe yes. It's complicated."

Anne signalled to the waitress, and to Bella she said, "I've got all the time in the world."

Bella began to explain. She found it a relief to be able to

tell somebody about it. That was what they always said, she told herself: a confession to somebody else was often the best way to relieve the burden of guilt. She had read an article in a magazine about that and had not paid much attention. Magazines were full of unsolicited advice about what one should do and what one should not do; she was above all that, and yet now she remembered it.

At the end of Bella's explanation, Anne was wide-eyed. "You *planted* your father's clothes . . . *planted* them? To get rid of her?"

Bella nodded. "Yes. Awful, isn't it?"

Anne seemed embarrassed. She hesitated, being unwilling to offend her friend, but then she said, "Yes, not very good." She gave Bella a searching look. "You aren't making this up?"

"I wish I was."

Anne leaned forward. "Why? Why did you want to get rid of her? Was she very strict?"

Bella shook her head. "Not at all. No, I thought that she was somehow going to take my father away from me."

Anne frowned. "As in . . . run away with him?"

Bella nodded. "Something like that. I saw her as a threat."

"And was she?"

"Was she going to take him away? I don't think so. I think she was totally innocent. I didn't really understand what was going on." She paused. "My mother might have – and I say *might* – have felt that she was after my father, or that my father was after her. I might have picked something up from her. But I very much doubt if there was anything to it."

"Yet you couldn't be sure?"

"Not really."

"Mind you, you were . . . how old?"

"Not quite nine."

"Well . . . Who hasn't done terrible things when they were not quite nine? My brother shot our neighbour's pet rabbit with a pellet gun – through the head – when he was seven. Deliberately. Then he buried the body in the garden so that he wouldn't be found out. But he put a little cross on the grave, and so my parents knew there was something going on. That was rather stupid of him."

Bella smiled. "Criminals make mistakes."

"You can say that again. But you know something? He forgot about it, and now he denies that it ever happened. But I remember it quite clearly."

Bella looked rueful. "I almost forgot about this. Then I remembered – just a few minutes ago, actually. Sitting here, I remembered every detail."

The waitress brought Anne's order of a cup of tea and a scone. "I still feel hungry," Anne remarked. "After the War and not having much to eat, and shortages going on and on. You'd think they could have stopped rationing sugar by now."

Bella had her doubts. "I heard that won't happen for ages. But people won't put up with it forever." She looked at Anne's scone – at the generous portion of butter and jam beside it on the plate. "At least we can come to places like this if we get too famished."

Anne took a sip of her tea. "This governess, this Miss . . ."

"Miss White."

"Yes, what happened to her? She left Ceylon?"

"She said she was going to. I think she was going to India. Presumably she's back from there now."

"Do you think she got married? Do you think she's living somewhere with a husband and family and has forgotten all about it? That's perfectly possible, you know."

Bella considered this. "I doubt if she got married. She was a real old maid, you know."

"Bluestocking?"

"Yes. I heard my mother talking about her with my father. She was saying that she thought that Miss White would never get married because no man would ever look at her. I remember her describing her as *plain*, and I remember wondering what plain meant."

"Poor woman. It must be dreadful to be somebody like that – not to have *any* chance of finding a husband."

"You can become a schoolteacher, of course. There's always that. Or end up looking after ancient parents."

Anne rolled her eyes. "Imagine! What a fate. I would hate to be an old maid. I'd hate it."

"You won't be," said Bella. "You'll find somebody really romantic. A bit like Rimbaud, perhaps."

"Good God, no. Not him."

"Well, somebody else then. But a Frenchman, nonetheless, with an open-topped sports car and a house in the South of France. And I'd visit you in your villa, and there would be tennis parties and drinks on the terrace, and your handsome husband would be drifting around lighting people's cigarettes for them, pouring them drinks and so on. Just think of it. He'd be wearing tennis whites – and you'd have wonderful clothes – whole wardrobes of them – and a maid who would look after just you, and it would be just perfect."

Anne picked up her scone and examined it. "I love these scones – I just love them. Scottish scones are far nicer than English scones." Her gaze shifted to Bella. "But what are you going to do? Anything?"

When Bella did not answer immediately, Anne continued, "If you feel bad about it – and you say you do – then why not get in touch with her? Write her a letter. Say that the whole thing's been preying on your mind and you wanted to apologise."

"I don't know. I really don't know."

"She would hardly reject the apology – unless she's become a fearful old battle-axe."

"She might have."

"Yes, she might. But what have you got to lose? If you feel bad about it – if your conscience is troubling you, then you've got nothing to lose, surely, by telling her how sorry you are that . . ."

". . . that I wrecked her life?"

Anne made a dismissive gesture. "Oh, come on – you haven't wrecked anybody's life. And who knows – maybe it was a good thing for her to leave Ceylon. Think of what might have happened to her when the Japanese invaded?"

"They didn't. They sent planes. They bombed it a bit. But they didn't invade. It wasn't like Burma or Malaya."

"All right. But it couldn't have been much fun being stuck somewhere like that for the whole war. You would have been wondering every day if something like Singapore was going to happen all over again. And then you'd be in one of those camps when people died every day from cholera and beriberi and so on and were as thin as skeletons – you'll have seen the pictures." Anne looked at her intently. "Honestly, Bella, you probably did her a favour."

Bella had to smile. "A good friend is somebody who makes all the things you do look good. You've just shown you're a good friend."

"But what I said is true."

Bella toyed with the last crumbs of her scone. "I suppose I could," she said.

"Get in touch?'

"Yes."

"How?"

"I'll ask Professor White for her address."

Anne rubbed her hands together. "Good. That's settled, then. Let's talk about something else."

"Such as?"

"Boys. I mean, men, I suppose."

Bella laughed. "There's not much to be said about them, you know."

Anne affected a disappointed expression. "I think you're right. I've been hoping that I'd discover that men were infinitely fascinating, but the truth is, they're not."

"Oh well, let's talk about them anyway."

"*Faute de mieux*," said Anne. "In the absence of anything better."

"*Faute de mieux*," echoed Bella.

2

Richard Writes

She had seen Richard three or four times since they had both been back in Scotland. Heather had found her way back from Ceylon on a troopship returning from India in 1943, her husband having stayed in Ceylon. She had visited Bella at her aunt's house, a month or two after her arrival in Scotland, bringing Richard with her. He was fourteen then; she had been taller than he was when they had last seen one another – now the growth spurt that comes upon teenage boys had reversed that, and she found herself looking up into hazel eyes that she had not really noticed before. She thought he was beautiful, which was something that she had not imagined she would ever think of a boy – but he was. He was tall, and lithe, and he smiled at her gently. "I'm really sorry about your mum and dad," he said. "I'm so sorry."

She looked away, but thanked him.

"The Japs," he said, and shook his head.

"Yes," she said. She did not know what she could add, and so she asked him about his school, and he told her that it was in the hills of Perthshire and they had a pipe band and he played rugby. At weekends the boys were encouraged to hike in the hills. He often called in with a friend at a nearby farm and helped the farmer with the sheep. It was more fun than walking, he said, and the farmer's wife gave them homemade ginger beer and carrot cake. They had a housemaster known as Toffee Martin who collected stamps and produced Gilbert and Sullivan operettas. The headmaster was called the Warden, although the boys called him the Warder, because some people said there was not much difference between a boarding school and a prison. He did not think that, though, and he was happy there. Was she happy where she was?

She told him that she was. Her form teacher was kind to her, especially after what had happened, and the work was not at all hard. She was ahead of the other girls in mathematics and history, and even further ahead when it came to geography. Miss White had drilled her thoroughly in rivers of the world, but had also included hills and some plains. She knew all about contour lines, which some of the other girls had yet to grasp. "Some of them are really stupid," she said. And he, nodding in agreement, had said, "And some boys at my school are pretty dim too. Not all of them – just some."

She saw him again two years later, when Heather had invited her and her aunt to have tea with her in Jenners, the large department store on Princes Street. Richard had been allowed to join them in Edinburgh, and they talked to one another while the adults chatted. The following year, she met him at a dance held at the school. A busload of boys from his school had been brought down to dance with the girls under the watchful eyes of the teachers. They had danced every dance together – they were mostly Scottish reels – and at the end of each set he had held her hand slightly longer than strictly necessary. She had blushed, and hoped that her hand did not feel clammy to him. No boy would like a clammy girl, she felt.

He wrote to her very occasionally – usually just a

postcard, on which a few not very informative sentences would be scrawled. His handwriting was untidy, but that, she thought, was because he was a boy. That was how they wrote, she believed.

In his final year of boarding school he sent a postcard that showed a picture of Crieff Hydropathic Institution, a large spa-like hotel. His father had returned from Ceylon for good, he told her, and they were having a family holiday at the Hydro. He was doing some clay-pigeon shooting and riding. His father went for long walks and drank whisky with various "moustachioed characters in their bedrooms, as they have to smuggle the whisky past the hotel authorities in cabin trunks" while his mother, who liked swimming, was doing fifty lengths a day. "She's in the pool for hours," he said, and then he went on to write, "and the smell of chlorine wafts after her in the corridors. I try to disown her, at least until she has showered and washed it off. I have applied to study medicine at Edinburgh University. It has a very famous medical school, as I think you know. I can't wait to go there."

She did not hear from him again until the day after her conversation with Anne in the tearoom, when a letter arrived. It had been addressed to her care of her aunt, who had sent in on to St Andrews.

"I'm sorry to have been out of touch," he wrote. "You know how it is. But I've been thinking about you – I promise! Not all the time, but at least sometimes . . . I'm in my second year of medicine. I think I told you that was what I wanted to do – well, now I'm doing it. The first year was biochemistry, physiology and anatomy. Anatomy is when you decide whether you've made the right decision or whether medicine's not for you. There was a chap at my table – six of us work on each cadaver (as we call the body)

– and he passed out twice. Stone cold. He couldn't take it, and he went off to study chemistry. I didn't mind it too much – in fact, it's quite interesting. Except for the smell of formaldehyde. I don't like that.

"I play rugby. I'm not all that good, but I've scraped into the University Second XV, and we're coming to play in St Andrews next month – on the first Saturday. If you get this letter in time, can we meet afterwards? Some of us are going to be staying over until Sunday, and I thought you might like to come to a party. There's always a party afterwards. You could bring a friend if you like (a girl, please!)"

She wrote back and said that she would be there to watch the game – "I'm a bit hazy about the rules, but that doesn't matter, I think" – and that she and her friend, Anne, would love to come to the party afterwards. He sent a postcard back, which said, "Great. Can't wait. Love, R." *Love, R . . .* She knew she should not read too much into that, but she did. *Love, R.*

The party went on past midnight. Richard was separated from the friends who had promised accommodation for the night, and Bella and Anne invited him back to the Hall, which he had to enter through a side window. He spent the night on a mattress of blankets on the floor of their room. Bella lay awake, aware of his presence just a few feet away; he had fallen asleep quickly, for he was tired after the game of rugby and the party that followed. She saw the moonlight upon him; he had gone off to sleep quickly; she saw the exposed shoulder and the hair that fell across his brow, and she felt an ache of wonder and possession, and a sense of privilege that this should happen to her, that he should come back into her life from a childhood that she had somehow put out of her mind because it had been so strange and had ended so sadly.

After that, they saw one another regularly. The years slipped by with the transience that years at university always have. His course was a demanding one, and he had to spend the university vacations working in hospitals in other parts of Scotland. Nothing was ever spelled out, but they both seemed to accept that whatever shape their future might have, they would spend it together. They became lovers, and he gave her a ring. He said, "I know this is old-fashioned, but I would prefer it that way." And she kissed him, and slipped it on the finger on which an engagement ring should go, and said that she was old-fashioned too. Her aunt noticed the ring, and although Bella said nothing about it, she said, "That's the right thing to do. Nobody disapproves – as long as there is a ring."

He said, "I love you so much, Bella. I've loved you right from the beginning, you know – when we were children. Right from then."

She said, "I know that," although she had not really known. She had hoped that this would be so, but she had not known.

She had never spoken to Professor White about Ceylon – she had felt awkward about it and feared that Miss White might have told him what had happened. If she had, then he might harbour a very low view of the people who had mistreated her so badly. So she remained silent through the four years of her university course.

At the graduation ceremony she felt the absence of her parents. Most of the other students had their parents there; she had her aunt and Richard. They sat in the hall, and as the academic procession entered – the professors in their colourful robes – everybody stood up and sang the 'Gaudeamus'. She knew the words well, as the university choir often sang it, along with other songs from the *Scottish Students' Song Book: Gaudeamus igitur, juvenes dum sumus*: let us rejoice while we are young.

The university laid on a reception afterwards, and she found herself talking to Professor White. She introduced Richard, who was standing next to her, and Richard said, "We've known one another since we were very young, back in Ceylon."

She drew in her breath and prepared to say something to take the conversation in a different direction. But the professor had raised an eyebrow. "Ceylon? You were in Ceylon, Bella? You never mentioned it."

She mumbled something about not having thought anybody would be interested.

"A lovely country, I believe," said Professor White. "My daughter was there for a short while. She spent more time in India, but she was in Ceylon just before the War. She was a governess."

Now it was too late. Richard said, "But Bella had a governess, didn't you, Bella? Miss . . ."

And then he remembered that she had said, "This is Professor White."

Professor White was looking at her with intense interest. "You don't mean that . . ."

She had no alternative. "I think it must have been your daughter. It never occurred to me." This sounded lame – she could tell that even as she spoke, but he did not appear to notice.

"What an extraordinary coincidence." He smiled broadly. "She loved her time there. But I believe she lost touch with the family – I suppose that means with you and your parents . . ."

She felt relieved. *She loved her time there* . . .

Richard explained. "I'm afraid that Bella's parents lost their lives in the War."

Professor White reached out and touched her forearm gently. "I'm so sorry. I wasn't aware."

"That's all right. I should have told you."

Bella felt her heart beating hard within her. She gave her empty teacup to Richard and addressed Professor White. "How is she? Your daughter? Where . . ."

"She's down in Suffolk," Professor White said. "She married a race-horse trainer. They have a stables, or whatever you call it. He's very successful." He smiled in a self-deprecating way. "I don't know a thing about race-horses, but I gather he's one of the top people in the field. He takes horses from all over the place and trains them for the big races – Cheltenham, the Grand National – that sort of thing."

Bella laughed. "Goodness."

"Yes, I must say that it's not what I had expected would happen to her, but there we are. Life has a way of taking unexpected directions." He paused. "I'm sure she'd love to hear how you're doing. Would you like her address?"

Bella nodded.

Professor White seemed pleased. "I'll drop her a note and say that you might be getting in touch. I'm sure she'll be pleased."

Bella looked at Richard. He had detected something in her manner that was a warning, but he was not sure what it was. It had been a long time ago. There had been some row or other about Miss White, but he could not remember what it was. But Bella did: she remembered that he had urged her to do something to get rid of Miss White – that was how she remembered it. He was party to what happened, even if he seemed unaware of his complicity. And now he had brought up the whole issue by blurting out to Professor White that they had known one another since Ceylon and that she had had a governess. This was his fault.

He said to her, "I can tell that you're cross with me."

She turned away. She did not want to spoil the day of her graduation with a row, and so she said, "I'm not cross with you. Just leave it."

But he was persistent. "How was I to know that you didn't want him to know about . . . about everything – Ceylon, Miss White, all that? How was I to know?"

She bit her lip and struggled to contain her feelings, which were ones of resentment and anger. He was right: he was not to have known, but that did not make it any easier for her.

"I don't think we should discuss it," she said. "Let's talk about something else."

"You don't have to be in touch with her," he said. "She won't necessarily be expecting it, even if he tells her that you'll be writing to her. People promise to do things they never do. Nobody expects much from other people."

She looked into his eyes. "I have to. I should have done it a long time ago. I have to apologise for what I did. Properly. As an adult."

He found it hard to understand. "We all do stupid things. We don't have to carry them with us for the rest of our lives."

"We don't have to, but we do. There's a difference."

He met her gaze with a challenge of his own. "Do you really think that? Do you really think that we have to go over the past and sort out all the things that have happened – all the things that we've done that maybe we shouldn't have done, or that we've done badly?"

"I think we do. Yes."

"Well . . ." He shrugged. He could not imagine what it

would be like to have the entire weight of history on one's shoulders.

"I know it may be hard," she said. "But we have to do it."

"And what else do you think you need to apologise for?"

She thought for a few moments before she responded. "For the whole thing? The whole British Empire? Sometimes I think that we'll need to say sorry about that sometime. India, for instance. And other things. Taking people's countries away from them."

He stared at her. "But that was just the way it was."

"Maybe. But that doesn't make it right."

"There's nothing *right* about the way the world is," he said. "The world is all about power and control and money. That's the way it is. And whether or not anybody has to say sorry depends on how they behaved while all that was happening around them."

"I don't think we should argue," she said.

"I wasn't arguing. I was just saying."

She looked at her hands. "If I went down to see her, would you come with me?"

"To see Miss White? Down in . . . where did he say?"

"Suffolk."

"Yes, down there – you want to go and see her?"

"I do."

"If she asks you?"

"Yes, of course. I'll write to her and ask whether we can come and see her. How long would it take to drive down?"

He had a car of which he was inordinately proud. "In my car . . . eight hours? Maybe less. It depends on the roads."

"We could find a hotel near her place – wherever that is. Could you take a few days?"

He was in his final year now, and he still had a couple

of examinations to sit. "After my exams, yes. I'll have three weeks before I start my first house job at the Infirmary."

"Shall we do it, then?"

"Yes. If you think it'll help."

"I don't know whether it'll help, but I feel I have to do it."

"Then you should."

The crisis had passed. He bent forward and kissed her. "I am so proud of you," he said.

"For doing this? For going to see Miss White?"

He laughed. "No, for getting a degree in English." And then added, "But also for that. For being brave and knowing what the right thing is to do."

"If it is the right thing," she said. "Which it may not be."

"What counts is wanting to do what you think is the right thing."

"Perhaps," she said, and then added, "Perhaps not."

She looked at her watch. They were to meet her aunt at a nearby hotel, where the three of them would have a celebratory meal together. She said, "You know those two old dolls I keep in my room? You know the ones?"

"Li what's-his-name and his friend, Po . . ."

"Li Po and Po Chü-i. Yes, them."

"I like the way women keep their old friends – their teddy bears, their dolls and so on."

"They've been with me all my life. I could hardly get rid of them. Anyway, I think I'll take them down to Suffolk with us when we go. She'll remember them, I think. It would be nice to show them to her – to remind her."

"That's fine," he said. "There's enough room in the car for four."

3

Forgiveness by the East River

The house stood away from a cluster of trees, oaks by the size of them, and it had the feel of a house that had been there as long as the land itself, as rocky protuberances sometimes seem to be – punctuation marks to the landscape's own story, rather than impositions.

Richard slowed the car as they drew off the road and started along the undulating driveway. "What a place," he muttered.

It took Bella a few moments to respond. "Who would have imagined it? Miss White, of all people, ending up in a place like this."

"Ordinary people can live in very grand houses," said Richard.

"That must be the stable-yard," said Bella, pointing to a low cluster of buildings some distance from the main house.

"Looks like it," said Richard.

And as he spoke, a line of half a dozen horses appeared from round the corner of one of the buildings, each ridden by a crouched figure, slightly humped, in the way of jockeys, rocking in harmony with the horse's gait.

"Exercise," said Richard. "They take them for a gallop every morning."

He slowed down again as they watched the horses move through a gate and then, in unison, start off at a canter across a stretch of ground reaching towards the horizon. He turned to her, "I never asked you: can you ride?"

She shook her head. "No. I don't mind horses, but I'm not sure that I see the point."

He smiled. He already had, she thought, that cheerfully brisk manner of the doctor he was on the cusp of becoming. She liked that, and understood why doctors had to be that way. It was either that or tears: a choice that the rest of us also faced, although not as pressingly or constantly. "Of being a horse, or of riding one?"

"Oh, I can see what the point of being a horse is – the same as the point of our being us. But riding? Well, it's quite a long way to fall. My father had a horse in Ceylon. Did yours?"

Richard nodded. "He had very bad-tempered horse. I remember how he'd look at you from the corner of his eye, hoping that you'd get within kicking distance. He bit too. I never worked out what his problem was, other than that he hated people."

They were approaching the house, and both fell silent.

"Georgian," muttered Bella. "Look at the proportion of the windows – and the doors. The Golden Ratio."

Richard frowned. "What?"

"The ratio between height and length. This house looks perfect because of that proportion." She swallowed. "I'm a bit nervous, Richard."

"She seemed very friendly on the phone. She said she had been looking forward to our visit for weeks."

"She said that," agreed Bella. "But do you think she meant it? She was always polite. Maybe she was just being polite."

Richard laughed. "Let's see. If it's a disaster we can just go." He glanced at her, saw her nervousness and rapidly said, "But it won't be a disaster, anyway. It's going to be . . ." He searched for the right word. "Interesting."

She pursed her lips. The journey here had been a long one. Eight hours, as he had predicted, in one sense; in another it had been a journey of years.

She barely recognised Miss White, who had fleshed out. The thin face on which the rouge had been caked, the high forehead, the fragile, schoolmistress demeanour – all those had gone, to be replaced by an almost sybaritic figure and the confident, no-nonsense bearing of the countrywoman. They used the word *country* to describe such people, Bella thought – her aunt used it, usually with disapproval.

"My Bella!"

Miss White rushed forward, arms wide open, to embrace her. Bella stood where she was, flustered. Her instinct was to dodge the charge, but she steeled herself and found Miss White all about her, her arms briefly on her shoulders, then moving down, caressing in ownership. Bella saw Richard grin, pleased, if slightly embarrassed, by this show of affection.

And then the compliments. "So grown up! But of course you are. It would be strange – very strange – if you were still nine." And then, following an appraising glance at Richard, "And such a handsome young man. But of course he would be, with you having become such a beauty. My goodness! You won't remember me, Richard, but . . ."

"I do remember you. From the club. And when I came to the house once or twice."

"You must have a good memory."

Bella said, "You're looking so well yourself, Miss White."

"Me? Oh, goodness, I just get by the same as ever. I get lots of exercise, of course, with everything that goes on here." She paused. "And please, it's Lavender – not Miss White."

She took Bella's hand and drew her towards the door that led from the hall into the drawing room. Pictures of horses, thought Bella, and expensive china in a display cabinet; a table with silver objects; a grand piano, lid up; a wood fire in the grate of a marble fireplace.

"This is a lovely place," said Bella.

"You think so? Yes, it is. Brian lived here with his mother before we married. Well, we shared the house with her for a couple of years. Then she died."

Bella glanced at Richard, but he was looking out of the window.

"Will you be able to stay for lunch?" asked Miss White. "I'm so sorry that you're going to have to head back up the road and can't stay a night or two."

"Richard has to get back."

"Of course he does. I'm sorry, too, that Brian can't be here. He's in Ireland at the moment. He comes back the day after tomorrow."

"Horses?"

"Yes, of course. Everything is horses here. He trains some of the Irish horses as well as horses from . . . well, all over the place. We're getting some from France now."

Miss White left to fetch a tea tray.

"Amazing," whispered Richard. "They're obviously pretty well-off."

Bella raised a finger to her lips in a gesture of silence, but whispered back, "She's changed."

Richard nodded. "See?" he said.

She was not sure what he meant. He might have meant

that everybody changed; he might have meant that we remembered things the wrong way round; he might have meant that memory faded, and with good reason.

Over tea, Miss White said, "I was so sorry to hear about your parents. I should have written – I meant to, but well, the War, and I was in Calcutta. Then Delhi for a short time before coming back. So much happened."

Bella said, "Thank you. Don't worry about not having written." She paused. "I remember you had friends in Calcutta."

She remembered something else, and reached for the bag she had brought in with her.

"Something to show me?" asked Miss White.

Bella took out Li Po and Po Chü-i and held them out towards Miss White.

Miss White's eyes widened. "Well, well, your dolls. Those two. There they are." She did not offer to take them.

"I thought you might like to see them."

"Of course." Miss White turned to Richard. "They went everywhere back in those days. Bella and those two were inseparable."

"Still are," said Richard, smiling. "But I'm not the jealous type."

They all laughed. Except Li Po.

Miss White became serious. "So much happened."

Bella nodded. "I remember my mother's fall."

Miss White inclined her head. "Of course. That was terrible." She paused. "You do know that it was an accident, don't you? You know that?"

"Yes, of course," said Bella.

"And then there was that awful moment with the snake," said Miss White. "Do you remember that?"

"I remember that," muttered Bella. "You saved my life."

Miss White laughed. "Hardly."

"But you did," protested Bella. And now she realised that she would have to say what she had come to say. She should not put it off, but should say it now. "And then I went and . . . well, I think I did something really bad. I think I wanted you to lose your job."

"Oh, nonsense," said Miss White quickly. "You did nothing of the sort."

"I've wanted to say sorry for a long time," said Bella. "I tried back then, but I was too young."

"Of course you were," said Miss White. "And you had nothing to apologise for. I'm the one who should be saying sorry. For not saying goodbye properly. For not staying in touch with you." She hesitated. "If I had stayed in touch, I might have been able to speak to you about what happened."

They looked at one another in silence. Then Miss White said, "It's strange, isn't it, how we carry some bits of the past with us for a long, long time – when we don't really need to."

Bella bit her lip. She had not been prepared for this, although now, when she came to think about it, she was not sure what she had expected. She had simply not thought it through.

She started to say something, but Miss White interrupted her. "Various things happened, you know . . ." She stopped and glanced at Richard, surreptitiously, thought Bella.

"I find it hard to speak about all this," Miss White said suddenly, and then, turning to Richard, "Richard, I know this will sound rude, but I feel that I know Bella really rather well and . . . well, you and I don't really know one another, and . . ."

Richard looked taken aback, but only for a moment or two. Then he became tactful. "Of course," he said, and then

added, "Of course," as he rose to his feet. "May I go outside
and see the . . . the . . ." He pointed.

Miss White was relieved. "The stables? Yes, certainly.
There'll be something going on – there usually is. Do you
like horses?"

"A bit," said Richard, and they all laughed.

He left, and the two of them were alone. Miss White shot
a glance at Bella. She was still hesitant, and she looked at the
door through which Richard had left as if half expecting him
to reappear. Then she turned to Bella.

"This is not easy for me," she said.

Bella nodded. "Nor for me. I was really anxious about
coming, you know, and . . ."

Miss White interrupted her. "I have to tell you something,
and yet I'm very worried about it. I'd like you to make me a
promise first, if you don't mind."

Bella looked puzzled. "Do you want me to keep it secret?
Of course I'll do that."

"I don't want you to mention any of this to Richard."

Bella frowned. But then she said, "Yes, all right. If that's
what you want."

"It is." She paused. "I know that you two are engaged.
And I know that some people say you should have no secrets
from the person you marry. But, believe me, there are some
things married people should keep from one another. We
all have to have little private areas – otherwise . . ." She
shrugged. "It becomes unhealthy otherwise. The soul is
too . . . too exposed, I suppose."

Bella was not sure whether she agreed or not. What
secrets did Miss White have in mind? Of course there were
things you should not talk about, even to the person you were
going to marry. What went on in a previous relationship,
for instance, the intimacy: nobody would talk about that to

anybody, surely, even if they were planning to get married. And quite rightly so. But was Miss White talking about something like that?

Bella waited.

"How well do you know Richard's mother?" Miss White asked.

Bella took a few moments to reply. "I know her well. She's been very kind to me."

It seemed to Bella that this was not the answer that Miss White was hoping for. "Why do you ask?"

Miss White looked away briefly. Now facing Bella, she shook her head, as if she regretted – in advance – what she was about to say. "This is so difficult for me."

Bella felt concern now. This was why she did not want Richard to be present. She decided to be bold. "It won't make any difference, you know. Nothing you say will affect how I feel about Richard." She paused. "And why should it? Even if you tell me something about his mother that . . ." She struggled. ". . . that I don't like – even if you do that, it won't make any difference to Richard and me."

Miss White winced. And then, suddenly, it came out – in a torrent. "I know that you thought that I was . . . I was *involved* with your father, and that you wanted your mother to think that. You wanted that so that I should have to leave. And all the time it wasn't me at all, it was Heather, Richard's mother. It was her. I knew that because I had found out about them. I wasn't going to do anything – or say anything either – because I thought it wasn't any of my business."

She looked at Bella, as if to check that her story, thus far, was being believed. And then she continued, "But the problem was that Heather knew that I knew. I came across them together, you see, on a walk, near the club.

They thought they were alone, but I was further down the path, and I saw them. She saw me, but your father did not. She knew that I knew, but I don't think she can have told him."

Bella held her breath. Her father had not been a major figure in her life – she had decided that after his death. She remembered him fondly, but he had been somewhat distant. He was always there, he was a reassuring presence, but he had never said all that much to her. That was such a curious conclusion to reach about a parent, she knew that, but it was what she felt. He had never really said very much. And there were many men like that, she felt, especially in those hills, in those days. They did not say very much.

Miss White had more to add. "You may be wondering how I knew this? You may wonder how I knew what Heather did next."

Bella shook her head, but said nothing. She was not sure what to think.

"Heather decided," Miss White went on, "that she would deflect any suspicion from herself by convincing your mother that there was something between your father and me. Which there wasn't, you know – there never was anything – anything – like that. Never.

"So she encouraged your mother to suspect me. That would also have the result of getting rid of me as a threat." She looked at Bella, and Bella knew that what she was being told was true. Miss White could not look at her as she looked at her now and be lying. It was impossible.

"It worked, of course. If I had protested and gone to your mother to tell her about their affair, what do you think your mother would have thought? She would have thought that I was accusing Heather to discredit her. And it would have made sense for me to do that, wouldn't it – if I had indeed been involved with your father. But I wasn't, and I had no desire to interfere. So I decided to go meekly – as people like me were meant to do.

"But . . . but, Bella, I did go to see Heather just before I left the country. I was staying with some friends of mine, and they took me. I went to see her, and a most unexpected thing happened. She broke down. She told me everything. She explained what had happened. She said that the affair was over now, and she felt that she had done me a terrible wrong. She offered to go to speak to your mother and confess everything."

Bella stared at Miss White. She struggled to make sense of what was being said. Why would Heather do this?

Miss White had anticipated her question. "Guilt," she said. "She felt guilty. And that, I feel, is why I can tell you about this. Because Heather was, I suppose, merely human. The same as everybody was. We were all human. And some of us did terrible things, and others did just foolish things. She felt sorry for what she had done. And you mustn't think badly of your father, because he went back to your mother, and men in those circumstances . . . well, they were terribly lonely, and it was difficult in so many ways and . . ." She shrugged. "Who amongst us hasn't done *something*?"

Bella waited for Miss White to say more, but she seemed to have reached the end of her revelations.

"Why did you tell me this?" she asked.

Miss White hesitated, but then she spoke with firmness. "Because I didn't want you to think that it was me all along. I didn't want you to believe that the person entrusted with looking after you should have abused her position. Because, I suppose, I have my pride."

Bella looked thoughtful. "I can see that."

"Those other things," Miss White said. "Those incidents.

The snake was complete chance. Snakes can get anywhere. Things like that can confuse the picture."

It came back to Bella. "And when your gun went off?"

Miss White stared at her.

"When you were packing? At the end? Your gun went off."

There was a clock in the hall. It was ticking. Somewhere, elsewhere in the house, from the kitchen, perhaps, the clatter of plates.

Miss White's voice was distant. It was tiny. "I fired it," she said. And then added, her voice becoming stronger with each sentence, "I'm so sorry. I can't believe that I did. Your father barged into my house, and I suddenly felt a welling up of real anger. Here was a man. We were all women. We had to do their bidding. We were adjuncts. They had affairs. They ran the place. It was them, them, them. And we were nothing. So I took the gun from my suitcase, and I fired it in the air. Into the ceiling. And a bit of plaster came down and landed on his head. And I laughed. And that was it."

Miss White began to smile, and Bella did too – smiling at the release of tension, at the truth.

"That's all, Bella. That's the whole story."

"I see. Well, now . . ." She shrugged. She was not sure what she should say. But then she decided. "I think we can all forget about it now. Forget about everything. It's our secret. It won't make any difference to anything."

"In particular, don't hold anything against Heather."

"I don't."

"Just remember what it was like being a woman in those places," said Miss White. "It wasn't easy."

"And nor was being a man," said Bella.

"No, perhaps not."

When lunch was ready, they went outside to fetch Richard. He was talking to one of the stable hands, who was wearing a scruffy red jersey. The man smiled at Bella and revealed two missing front teeth.

"Kenny knows everything there is to know about horses," said Miss White.

Kenny's grin grew wider. A further gap appeared in his teeth.

Miss White led them back into the house, and into the dining room, where lunch was served by a stout middle-aged woman, introduced as the housekeeper. Miss White and Richard got on well, Bella noticed. There was something almost flirtatious in Miss White's manner, but Richard responded well, catching Bella's eye and smiling. *He's used to women like this,* Bella thought. And then she silently asked herself: why would I think that? *Women like this?*

Miss White spoke about Calcutta. "I had a very exciting time there, you know – after I left you. I joined the air force."

"You flew?"

Miss White laughed. "No. They didn't allow that."

"Most unfair."

Miss White agreed. "Yes, but I wouldn't have wanted to fly, anyway. I did administrative work. I had a lovely uniform and . . ." She smiled almost conspiratorially. "And the men were queuing up to take me out to dinner. I had a lovely time."

"And Delhi?"

"Even better," said Miss White. "I was given a job at Government House – right at the end. Just before the handover. I worked with Edwina Mountbatten. She did a lot out there, you know. They liked her a great deal. And when they left India there was a terrific crowd out to say goodbye."

Bella looked into her water glass. She had expected none of this. What had happened to the old maid-governess? Had that been nothing but a chrysalis?

"I went with the staff from Government House to Gandhi's funeral, you know," Miss White continued. "I shall never forget it. The vast throng of people. And the flowers. And the cries that Gandhi was now immortal, cries that rose up like the smoke off the pyre. And the millions of flowers. And the feeling that people had of wanting to live up to something that had just died before their eyes.

"It was through Edwina that I met Brian – once we were back in this country. I continued to have a role as a sort of social secretary, and I met Brian that way. We hit it off straight away, and we've been married now for four years."

Bella said, "I'm so glad you're happy."

Miss White looked into her eyes. And then she said, "Yes, I'm happy."

After coffee, they went out to the car, which was parked before the front door. Miss White embraced Bella and then kissed Richard on the cheek.

"Bless you," she said.

They drove down the drive. Bella turned her head to look back. Miss White was still standing there, watching them as they made their way towards the public road.

Her heart was full. She reached for Li Po and Po Chü-i, who had been sitting, arm in arm, on the back seat. She put them beside her. As she did so, she reverted to something she had not done for a long time – she addressed the dolls. It was a whisper and was not intended for Richard, who was busy anyway, adjusting the rear-view mirror.

"So that's Miss White," she said.

From beside her, a small voice said, "A likely story!"

Bella looked down. She saw Li Po's bad arm, with its

stitches. She thought, "You should forgive, you know."

But that, it seemed, was a difficult thing for a doll to do.

The roads were quiet, punctuated by the long shadows thrown by the hedgerows in the late-afternoon light. The Suffolk sky was large and empty, apart from wisps of white cloud here and there. Bella looked at Richard beside her. She reached out and touched his knee, gently. He smiled, and said, "Why did you do that?"

She shrugged. Why not? She loved him so much. She was so lucky.

She said, "I'm glad that Miss White is happy. I didn't think she would be, you know."

He said, "Happiness is an odd thing, isn't it? I'm not sure if you can set out to achieve it – it either happens to you or it doesn't."

Li Po listened. He muttered, "That's trite."

But nobody heard him, and dolls don't talk. Nor did he know that the following week he and Po Chü-i were going to be donated to a charity sale to raise money for the Royal Blind School.

Bella and Richard had three children – two girls and a boy. They asked their mother about Sri Lanka. She said, "It's hard to describe what it was like, and I was very young when I left it. I liked the people, though, and I'd love to go back one day."

Miss White had told Bella that she was happy, and that was true. She became happier still. She thought that when you looked at your life, you should not judge it just by one part, as we can all make mistakes. That's what she said one day to her husband, and he said, "You're right there, Lavender. Absolutely right. As always."

She named two of his racehorses after Li Po and Po

Chü-i. They were both very successful. Li Po won the Gold Cup at Cheltenham. Po Chü-i was sold to the Irish for a very large sum. Miss White used some of the proceeds to buy an eye-wateringly expensive set of early watercolours of views of Calcutta and the banks of the Hooghly. "I loved Calcutta," she said. "I loved it so much."

The dolls themselves were bought by a woman who was visiting Scotland from New York and who chanced upon the charity sale. She took them back to her fashionable apartment in Manhattan. They were placed in a glass case opposite a window that looked out over the East River. She knew everyone: Robert Lowell, Hemingway, Norman Mailer. They were admired by guests to the apartment, one of whom said one day, "This one has had an arm sewn back on. Look." And then she added, "If my arm ever falls off, I hope somebody's kind enough to sew it back on." That was Dorothy Parker.

The owner said, "Yes, you're right. I suspect there's a story behind that."

"Very possibly," said Miss Parker. "Most people whose arms fall off have a story."

Li Po just looked. He had nothing further to say, although he continued to observe. From his glass case he had a view, to the side, of the United Nations Building. He could see motorcades arriving on UN Plaza way down below on the street. He saw Kennedy; he saw Khrushchev. He saw everything.

He watched, while Po Chü-i dozed beside him, content with the warm sunlight that flooded through the window, yellow, textured, thick, like butter.

THE END

ABOUT THE AUTHOR

ALEXANDER MCCALL SMITH is one of the world's most prolific and most popular authors. His various series of books have been translated into over forty-six languages and have sold more than 30 million copies across the world. These include the *No. 1 Ladies' Detective Agency* series, the *44 Scotland Street* novels, the Isabel Dalhousie novels and the Von Igelfeld series. He also writes stand-alone novels, poetry, children's fiction and libretti for short operas.

Polygon

Polygon is an imprint of Birlinn Limited.

Birlinn is home to the finest writing from an impressive list
of authors. Our books range across nearly every subject
area, from history to sport, fiction to poetry, children's
titles to academic works.

Sign up to our newsletter to
keep up to date with all our latest
news and publications:
www.birlinn.co.uk/birlinn-newsletter

Birlinn Limited

Birlinn | Polygon | Arena Sport | BC Books | John Donald

Publishing in Scotland for the World.